THE GIRL WHO
KNEW TOO MUCH

THE GIRL WHO KNEW TOO MUCH

Margaret Pemberton

This title first published in Great Britain 1997 by
SEVERN HOUSE PUBLISHERS LTD of
9–15 High Street, Sutton, Surrey SM1 1DF.
First published in Great Britain 1974 under the
title *Rendezvous With Danger* by Macdonald and Jane's.
First published in the U.S.A. 1997 by
SEVERN HOUSE PUBLISHERS INC., of
595 Madison Avenue, New York, NY 10022.

British Library Cataloguing in Publication Data

Pemberton, Margaret
      The Girl Who Knew Too Much
      1.   Germany – Fiction
      2.   Romantic Suspense novels
      I. Title
      823.9'14 [F]

      ISBN 0-7278-5211-6

Typeset by Palimpsest Book Production Limited,
Polmont, Stirlingshire, Scotland.
Printed and bound in Great Britain by
Hartnolls Ltd, Bodmin, Cornwall.

For my Husband, Michael

Chapter One

I kicked off my sandals and sat down on the grassy hillside. Far below me the river wound in giant curves through the valley, the narrow road I had just travelled skirting its banks. On either side were green meadows knee-deep in summer flowers, rising gently into slopes of fir and pine. There wasn't a sound except for a bee lazily circling above my head.

I rolled over on to my stomach and reached idly for the binoculars. In the distance was a cluster of houses, the sun glinting on the shingled roofs and on the gilded spire of a tiny church. The surrounding fields were neatly tilled, and above them were orchards of apple trees, their boughs heavy with summer fruit. As I lowered my glasses I could see my parked car at the foot of the hill, almost hidden by the trees.

Niedernhall, the village where I was staying, lay some ten miles to the east, cupped in the sheltered fold of a small valley. It was encircled by crumbling walls, with each corner turreted and battlemented and a gable-ended watch-tower guarding the approach over the village bridge. The road across it was Niedernhall's only main street. It wound its way irregularly through the centre of the village, curving up the hill on the far side for three hundred yards or so, to die into a country path, amid fields thick with poppies and cornflowers. From here I intended lazily exploring a wild and lovely area, not often visited. Tourists either go south at Heidelberg to the castles of southern Bavaria, or continue on the autobahn to the more spectacular scenery of Austria.

I lay back, savouring the peace and tranquillity, happily unaware of the large car speeding down the road from Mannheim, its occupants as unaware of my presence high up on that deserted hillside as I was of theirs. Their arrival, when they rounded the bend in the road far below, would shatter my relaxed, restful holiday, and alter completely all my carefully arranged plans. But at that moment in time there was no sense of impending disaster, no intuition of what was to come.

A year ago I had stayed overnight in Niedernhall with a girl friend, en route for a fortnight in Innsbruck. Our holiday had been very successful, especially so for Charlotte, as it was while we were there that she met John Mammers whose wife she now was. However, his gain had been my loss, at least where holidays were concerned, and my bosom friend since schooldays had disappeared beneath a shower of confetti and good wishes to the north of England, leaving me without a companion. There was one compensation. It meant I was entirely free as to the choice of destination. Lazing in the country, doing nothing more exciting than exploring the medieval churches in the area, would not have pleased Charlotte. Her voice on the telephone had been incredulous.

'Susan, you can't be serious! That submerged hamlet, buried miles away in the depths of ancient Franconia?'

'Swabia.'

'Don't split hairs, it's all the same. You surely can't have forgotten the plumbing — it was straight from the Middle Ages. What on earth do you intend *doing* there, for heaven's sake?' Then, not waiting for a reply: 'I had a letter from Liza saying she'd wanted you to go with her to Spain, Sitges I believe, a little further south than Barcelona. Now wouldn't that be better? Plenty of sun and swimming instead of mouldering in the countryside.'

'I can assure you, Lottie, I shall be quite happy, and not mouldering as you so charmingly put it. I have the car and there are lots of places round about worth visiting.'

'You're not doing a retreat, are you?' Charlotte's voice was both suspicious and accusing. 'I thought you hadn't minded when Heathcliff returned to the States. If that's the cause of this "I want to be alone" kick . . .'

'If you are referring to Ian Davies,' I replied warmly, *'no*, I

2

am not doing a retreat and *yes*, I wasn't bothered when he returned to the States.'

'Your grammar is slipping,' she said complacently. 'Now I know I'm right. It's typical of you, going all nunlike and introspective. Now Spain would offer just the right diversion, take your mind off things.'

I laughed. 'No good, Lottie. You're way off beam. A lazy holiday without crowds of tourists swarming everywhere, doing what I want, when I want, will suit me fine. I'll send you a postcard.'

'Of a monastery?' I thought I heard her say, before replacing the receiver.

Well, it might not appeal to Charlotte, but it appealed to me, and as I had absolutely no one to consider but myself, I had returned to Niedernhall. On this, my second day there, I had as yet no cause to regret the decision.

I wasn't staying in a hotel but was bed-and-breakfasting at Frau Schmidt's, where we had stayed on our overnight stop the previous year. She lived in a small, stone-built cottage on the main street of the village. The upper walls bellied out over the cobbled pavement, covered with a thick, green creeper that spread its leafy tentacles over the mellowed stone and was probably responsible for holding the house in a vertical position. Petunias and fuchsias bloomed thickly in troughs on each window-sill and in pink and purple profusion in hanging baskets above the door. There were few concessions to the twentieth century, but the spartan interior was highly polished and the stone floors downstairs were scoured to a brilliant whiteness despite the stray hens that wandered desultorily in and out. There were two bedrooms on the second floor, each sparsely furnished with a dark wooden bed and a large chest for clothes. Handmade quilts and rugs brightened the sombre furniture, and there were jugs of summer flowers on the window-bottom.

Though I spoke hardly any German and Frau Schmidt's English was limited, she had made me feel as if my return was the highlight of her year and had fussed over me like a mother

3

hen its chick. I had shown her a photograph of a veiled and smiling Charlotte which threw her into raptures of delight, and she had raised my ringless hand, scolding and chastizing me for still being single.

I was only paying for bed and breakfast but she had insisted I take a packed lunch of thick-cut sandwiches, various cold sausages and home-made pastries with me when I left the house for the day. It would have fed a coachload of tourists let alone myself, but the fresh, clear air had sharpened my appetite and I was already looking forward to a picnic.

I raised my hand to shield my eyes from the sun as I looked around for a suitable place. I had left behind the thickly wooded lower slopes, and was now sitting on the grassy uplands without any protection from the sun's rays. From above came the distant sound of running water. It seemed to come from the crown of the hill, where a solitary group of pines stood silhouetted against the cloudless sky. The heat was intensifying and the shadows cast by the thick branches looked coolly inviting. Hitching my bag on to my shoulder I set off, the harebells and long grasses brushing pleasantly against my legs.

Ten minutes later I reached the summit and the welcoming shade. In the shadow of the grove of trees, a spring of water burst out of the ground, its source surrounded by small summer flowers of pink and yellow, tumbling in its narrow bed down the hillside. High up above a curlew wheeled and turned, and in the distance were small figures, hard at work in the vineyards.

Frau Schmidt had certainly done me proud. For fifteen minutes or so I sat there, leisurely eating my lunch and listening to the hypnotic surge of the water as it flowed past my feet, thinking of nothing in particular.

Just as I was about to put away my things, I saw the small dot of a car some miles to the north. The road curved out of view, but in an amazingly short space of time the car appeared again. I reached for the binoculars.

Even at this distance I could see it was moving dangerously

4

fast. Another curve of hills hid it from sight, and then, minutes later, it swept round the bend in the road directly below me. As it burst into my field of vision again, it lost control, spinning wildly across the road – one, two, three times – in complete circles. I sprang to my feet with a shout of horror, gripping the glasses. I couldn't see clearly for the thick, enveloping clouds of dust the skidding wheels had gouged from the road. With a slam I could almost hear, it rocketed into the base of the hill, shuddering from end to end, shattered glass flying in all directions. Then there was stillness, the only movement the panic-stricken flight of a flock of birds.

I was on my feet, half running, binoculars still glued to my face. The clouds of dust that had engulfed the car cleared, and with overwhelming relief I saw the driver's door open slowly, and the stout figure of a middle-aged man gingerly climb out. A second or so later, the other door opened, and his companion, a bald man, equally shaken, and feeling his arms and legs as if to reassure himself of their continued attachment, joined him. He leaned, head in hands, against the concertinaed wreck. The bonnet was now embedded deeply in the soft undergrowth on the wrong side of the road, the rear wheels lifted clear, spinning slowly to a stop.

I ran back to collect my bag, hastily stuffing the remnants of my picnic inside, then hurried as fast as I dare down the steep slope towards them.

I hadn't gone very far when a movement attracted my attention again. I slowed down and raised the binoculars, then stopped to focus better, puzzled. Instead of getting their breath back and recovering from what must have been a considerable shock, they were both agitatedly looking back along the road they had travelled. The bald man seemed to be shouting at his companion and was waving his fists at him. His friend, ignoring him, had turned his attention from the empty road and was now stamping his feet on the ground and dusting down his jacket and trousers. He was much smaller, with dark red hair and a magnificent moustache, dressed as an English country gentleman might, out for a day's shooting. As he

5

wiped his hands on his handkerchief, he saw my car parked on the verge some yards ahead.

I could see the precise moment its presence registered on him. He pointed it out to the still raging bald man and they both simultaneously began running towards it. I was just about to put the glasses back in my bag and increase my speed when, in utter amazement, I saw the stout man give a hasty look round, raise the bonnet of my car and lean over. The other stood, his hand shielding his eyes, scanning the surrounding hills, presumably for the car's rightful owner.

'What the . . . ' I began, waving furiously. For a moment he seemed to be looking straight at me and then his eyes moved, ranging further up the hill to where I had been sitting. Looking through the glasses I saw him quite clearly.

He was a burly man, of about forty to forty-five, with a heavily jowled face and full lips, and obviously not in the best of moods. It seemed impossible that he should fail to see me, but I was by now standing just above the belt of pines that grew thickly on the lower slopes, and no doubt from below was obscured from view. If the sun had been in the right direction it would have glinted on the lens of my glasses. As it was, his gaze, searching, slid up and over me.

Then, as I watched in utter disbelief, he gave up his search, turned, and began forcing my car door. Within seconds, as I stood helplessly watching, unable to do a thing to prevent him, he was in the driver's seat. *My* driver's seat. The bonnet was hurriedly slammed down and even while the puffing, tweeded and brogued figure of his associate was wrenching open the other door and clambering aboard, my little Morris was bursting into life and disappearing from my horrified gaze down the road.

For a second or so I just stared. Then as the full realization of what had happened sank in, I began running over the grassy slope and into the trees.

It didn't occur to me that racing down the hillside was not going to do any good whatever, but I was filled with blind fury. All I could think of was reaching the road in the shortest time possible. What I would do when I *did* reach it, marooned and without transport, I didn't stop to think.

Slipping and sliding I plunged steeply downhill, stumbling over gnarled tree roots and broken branches that lay murderously concealed in the thick undergrowth. This time I made what was practically a vertical descent, heedless of the sudden, hidden drops that threatened at any moment to result in a broken leg, or at the very least, a twisted ankle. The lower branches caught at my hair, their leaves slapping into my face, as I pushed my way through them. The hill had taken me an hour to climb. I emerged some thirty minutes later by the roadside, gasping for breath, legs scratched and bleeding.

My dress was covered with dark green stains and caked with dirt from the loose top-soil. I was already regretting my haste. Much good it had done me.

Here I was, stranded by a little-used roadside, with only the prospect of a lengthy walk of several miles to the nearest telephone, and *how*, for goodness sake, was I going to report the theft of my car in German? I groaned, remembering the arduous conversations I had carried out in the past. They had all been conducted with the aid of a phrase-book and sign language, and over nothing more involved than a request for directions or accommodation. The worst I thought, and how rightly, was yet to come.

With a gasp of exhaustion I collapsed on the grass verge.

Chapter Two

Five minutes went past, ten, and still the road remained empty. A few white clouds drifted across the sky and a light breeze fanned my cheeks, rustling through the long grass on either side of me, but bringing little comfort. With each minute that ticked away I thought of another problem.

Uppermost was my inability to explain my loss to the authorities. And what authorities? From what I'd seen of Niedernhall there wouldn't be the counterpart of the English village bobby. I plucked at the grass nervously. Just suppose I didn't get my car back, at least not within the next ten days, what then? Goodbye little Morris for ever? Why, oh why, didn't I read the small print on my insurances? Vainly I tried to remember precisely what was covered. Theft certainly . . . But in another country? Would they return the car to me once I was home in England? How would I *get* home, come to that?

Other worries came thick and fast. If the thieves were so careless with what was presumably their own property, how shabbily would they treat a car they had stolen? I looked at the wreck opposite me and groaned, envisaging my twenty-first birthday present lying similarly abandoned and damaged.

Anxiously I rose and began pacing up and down the grass verge. The scenery that surrounded me was as lovely as ever. The forest of pines that cloaked the hills in a dark green sea looked even more majestic from below than above, but I was no longer appreciative. The rhythmic surge of the water as it flowed languorously southwards some yards distant, the sun glinting on its shining surface, fell on deaf ears. The only sound I craved was that of a car engine.

At last it came. The distant hum grew stronger and I

stepped out into the road. The driver of the car braked hard, tyres screeching, halting a dozen yards away.

He slammed the door behind him and sprinted towards me, face ashen. I hadn't bargained on my rescuer filling the traditional role quite so adequately and was suddenly aware of my dishevelled appearance. Mentally I could hear Charlotte's '*Very* nice . . . '

'What the hell happened? Are you all right?' and then: '*Sind Sie* . . . ?'

'You're English,' I said tactlessly. 'Thank goodness. Yes, I'm all right. I wasn't in it actually.'

'Then who was and where . . . ' He spun on his heel in search of the dead and dying.

'*That* I only wish I knew.'

He raised his eyebrows. He was about twenty-seven or eight, with thick dark hair curling into the nape of his neck, and a tanned skin that must have had the aid of a hotter sun than the one we were now under. The eyes that looked at me questioningly were as dark as his hair and there was strength as well as sensuality in the curve of his mouth. He looked extremely self-confident and assured and was quite the most handsome man I had ever met. I found myself blushing like a schoolgirl.

'There's no need to worry. No one was hurt. Could you give me a lift to the nearest police station or, better still, Niedernhall? It's about ten miles away, further down the river . . . '

He waved my directions aside.

'I know it. I'll give you a lift with pleasure, if only to find out what you're doing with a crashed car you didn't travel in. Should prove interesting.'

'Oh, it's that all right.'

He grinned. 'My name is Stephen Maitland. I'm staying in Ohringen, practically the next village to Niedernhall.'

'I'm Susan Carter. I'm on holiday there, the idea being to get away from it all, though I didn't intend carrying it to quite such lengths.'

9

'I think,' he said dryly, 'you'd better explain.'

'I warn you, it's going to sound very far-fetched.'

'I'm very gullible,' he said, looking anything but.

'I'd parked the car, *my* car. at the roadside and had climbed the hill for a picnic, when that other car — ' I nodded disparagingly across the road — 'came tearing round the corner, lost control and ended up in the ditch. The two men who were in it got out, then, as I was on my way to *help* them for heaven's sake, they had the cheek to steal my Morris and continue on their merry way.'

He frowned. 'Very ungentlemanly. Did you get a good look at them?'

'Oh yes.' I patted the binoculars beside me. 'I saw it all through these. I'd certainly know them again, given the chance.'

'I shouldn't worry too much. I imagine they'll abandon the car pretty quickly.'

'I hope they don't do it in the same way they abandoned that.'

He laughed. 'I see your point. Well, first things first. Let me give you a lift to Niedernhall.'

Stephen Maitland's car was an open-topped Sprite and I pulled my scarlet headsquare out of my bag and knotted it securely beneath my chin. As I did so, there came the faint but unmistakable throb of a car. It was coming fast. The sound swelled, filling the still afternoon: whoever it was, was in a hurry. Seconds later a red Mercedes swept round the bend in the road. On seeing the crashed car, the drived pulled up sharply, halting in a cloud of dust beside us. A window was wound down and a young, fair-haired German leaned out.

'*Wie schwer ist ihr Wagen beschadigt?*'

Stephen replied, the car door swung open, and a tall, toughly-built young man, elegantly dressed in cream trousers, suede jacket and silk shirt, emerged. Adding Stephen's accent and GB plate together, he said: 'Perhaps I can be of assistance. I see there has been an accident. Gunther Cliburn is the name.'

Stephen shook the proffered hand. 'Stephen Maitland.' He

10

turned to me. 'And Miss Susan Carter.'

I smiled, and when I judged that Herr Cliburn had held my hand long enough, politely removed it. He reached inside his jacket for his cigarette case and offered it, saying to me as he did so: 'You were very lucky to walk out of that . . . ' He gestured towards the crashed car.

'I wasn't in it, thank goodness.'

'My apologies.' He steadied my hand as he lit the cigarette, and turned to Stephen. 'Did you skid?' These corners can be the -- how do you say -- the very devil.'

'I had the good fortune not to be in it either.'

Herr Cliburn raised an enquiring brow.

'Miss Carter had parked her car here,' Stephen went on by way of explanation, 'and then climbed the hill for a picnic. This car came along some little while later, crashed, and its two occupants took Miss Carter's car and disappeared. I arrived on the scene some ten minutes ago.'

'*Wirklich*?!' he said in astonishment. 'You are on holiday, Fraulein?'

'Yes. I'm staying at Niederhall.'

Herr Cliburn stared at me as if I had said in the land of green cheese. The hand holding his cigarette remained poised motionless in mid-air, then, recollecting himself, he said: 'But how extraordinary. How *very* extraordinary. I live there.'

It was my turn to be surprised. Munich yes. Niedernhall most definitely no.

'Perhaps I exaggerate a little,' he explained. 'I have a cottage there, a holiday retreat.' He looked down at his wrist-watch. 'I presume your first thought would be the police?'

I murmured agreement.

'Perhaps I could be of assistance. I know the police chief at Kunzelsau and also the local officer at Niedernhall. It would be no inconvenience for me to report the matter for you. Regrettably neither of these gentlemen speaks English. I feel sure your car will be found abandoned soon. I think this one here was stolen also, and the thieves simply joy-riding.'

11

'I hope you're right. Otherwise I'm stranded.'

Herr Cliburn laughed. 'That, Fraulein, I would not permit. Where do you stay in Niedernhall?'

'Frau Schmidt's, in the Ringstrasse, number twenty-six.'

'Then I will call there and inform you as to what the situation is,' he said, waving my feeble protestations aside. 'Can I ask if you saw the men?'

'Yes. I had my binoculars with me.'

Herr Cliburn dropped his cigarette stub and ground it out under his heel thoughtfully, then said: 'If you will give me all the particulars, Fraulein Carter.'

'Oh yes, of course.' I searched hastily in my handbag for pen and paper, scribbling down my car number and anything else I could think of, while Herr Cliburn and Stephen strolled over to the wrecked car, giving it a cursory examination. When I had finished, Herr Cliburn took the slip of paper with a smile.

'Irregular though it may seem, things will be quicker if I report this matter without your presence. I will say the affair has left you rather distressed. Thoroughness is a national trait and when it comes to dealing with foreigners, bureaucracy can be interminable. Herr Heller is a friend of mine and though no doubt your car will be found very soon, if you reported it yourself, he would feel obliged to go through all the formalities. You understand? As it is, I will see him and then I will call you. My telephone number is here. I am sure Herr Maitland will escort you back to Niedernhall.' He shook my hand again. 'Till later, Fraulein.'

With a nod of the head, he walked briskly back to his car. The Mercedes hummed into life and, with a wave of the hand, he disappeared round the bend and out of sight. I turned to Stephen.

'Is it a bit late to ask if I did the right thing?'

'A little. Perhaps if we go somewhere for a drink we can ponder on it for a while. If Herr Cliburn doesn't materialize, as promised, at your guest-house, then only a couple of hours will have been lost. I don't think it will make much difference to the outcome.'

'I suppose you're right. And he did seem to know what he was doing, didn't he?'

'Oh, indubitably,' said Stephen dryly, opening his car door for me. Without a backward glance at the empty car to our right, we headed down the dusty road.

'Are you holidaying by yourself?' he asked.

I nodded.

'Why this part of Germany? It's a little dull and quiet, isn't it?'

'Not at the moment,' I said wryly.

He laughed. 'It's not going to do you a bit of good hanging round Niedernhall waiting for James Bond to return. Ohringen is only minutes away. Would you like to go over there for a drink? I'm sure Christina would be delighted.'

'Christina?' I glanced at the ringless hands on the wheel.

'Christina runs the guest-house where I'm staying.' As he spoke he turned left, leaving the Niedernhall road.

If it hadn't been for all the doubts and worries in my mind I would have enjoyed that ride through the sloping fields of vines and lush woodland, with the warm sun on my back and the handsome Mr Maitland by my side. As it was, I kept glancing at my watch and wondering how Herr Cliburn was making out. Stephen had been right about my needing some diversion until he appeared again. Left to myself, I would have been a nervous wreck.

His guest-house turned out to be a pretty, chocolate-box chalet surrounded by a narrow wooden balcony ablaze with flowers. A few tables were set outside, covered with brightly checked cloths. An apple tree grew at the balcony's edge, and the leaves traced moving patterns on the tables below. There was no sign of any other visitors.

A black cat, who had been sunning himself on the balcony rail, leaped languidly to the ground at our approach and led the way, tail erect, up a couple of wooden steps into the surprisingly large hall. It was refreshingly cool inside. Bare stone slabs paved the floor and in the far corner was a half-mooned desk of dark oak. Behind it sat a girl of nineteen or twenty, in a white blouse and yellow dirndl skirt. As my high-heeled sandals rang metallically on the stone floor she raised her head, and on seeing Stephen, she smiled welcomingly. Her long brown hair was plaited and coiled in a halo round the top of her head. The well-defined brows were swept in smooth arcs over large green eyes, and though she wore no make-up her skin had an enviable lustre. The simple clothes she wore were the perfect foil to her fresh, natural beauty. Mentally re-assessing my own appearance after my scramble down the hillside, I felt I came off badly in comparison.

'Susan, this is Christina. You'll have no language problem as Christina spent three years in England, first as an au pair, then in the hotel trade. She came here last year when her father opened this guest-house. Christina, this is Susan Carter.'

We shook hands and she smiled shyly.

'Susan has just had her car stolen,' said Stephen matter-of-factly.

'No! But that is terrible.' Her expression changed to one of disbelief. 'Who would do such a thing? Is there anything I can do to help?'

'Not really. Someone is reporting it for me at the moment.'

'How did it happen?'

Briefly I told her about the crash and the two men, finishing with Herr Cliburn's appearance and offer of help.

'I expect you could do with a drink,' she said practically.

'An excellent idea.' Stephen looked questioningly at me. 'What would you like, Susan? A lager or something a little stronger?'

'A lager would be fine.'

Christina disappeared through the arched doorway and we walked out to the balcony, sitting at one of the tables beneath the trees. I took off my scarf and put it with my shoulder-bag on the ground. I leaned back, relaxing slightly.

'I feel as if I'm going to wake in a moment and find it's all a bad dream.'

'What did actually happen? Were they swerving to avoid an oncoming car?'

'No, there was nothing else on the road.'

'Except your Morris.'

'Except my Morris,' I agreed miserably.

'I think you'll find Herr Cliburn is right,' said Stephen, as he paused to take the drinks from Christina's tray. 'I mean, if the crashed car was their own, they'd hardly leave it like that, would they?'

'You mean you think the car was stolen?' asked Christina, pulling up a chair.

'Looks like it,' Stephen said.

'Whether it was their car or it wasn't they behaved in a most peculiar manner.' I shook my head, mystified. 'It was as if someone was following them.'

'You mean because they immediately grabbed your car?'

'That's one of the things, and also their behaviour when they got out of the car. They both seemed to be in a state of panic, looking back up the road as if they expected the hounds of hell to come galloping round the corner.'

'And all they got was Stephen,' said Christina, grinning.

I laughed. 'Yes. They couldn't have been being followed after all. It must have been a good twenty or thirty minutes before he came along and there was no other traffic in all that time.'

A bell rang and Christina sighed. 'Just when it is getting interesting. I shan't be long.' Unwillingly she rose from the table and disappeared inside the guest-house.

'I imagine any signs of panic you saw would be due to the crash,' Stephen said. 'They were both very lucky men. The car is practically a write-off. An experience like that would unnerve anybody.'

'I hope they treat my car with a bit more care.'

'After the shake-up they've just had, they'll be crawling along at thirty miles an hour now.'

'I hope so,' I said fervently.

'Trust my intuition. When they've got where they want to

go, they'll dump your car like a hot brick. It will be returned to you within hours. You see. The German police are very efficient.'

'I wouldn't know. I've never had anything to do with them. Do you know Germany well?'

'Not as well as I'd like to. That's why I'm pottering around here by myself. I've spent a lot of time in Munich this last year or so. I'm in advertising and the head office of our biggest account is there. This time I decided to combine business with pleasure and instead of heading back to London, hired a car and motored down here.'

'How many more days have you left?' I asked casually.

'That depends on when your car is returned. I could hardly disappear now, not knowing the outcome, could I?' He glanced at his watch. 'In fact, it's time we were making tracks for Niedernhall now. If your friend fails to appear, I'll run you straight to the police station myself.'

'Cross fingers it won't be necessary,' I said, picking up my bag and following him inside to say goodbye to Christina.

She was busy setting a tray for afternoon tea.

'Oh, you are not going so soon?' She pushed the tray to one side and hurried across to us. 'Perhaps Stephen could bring you back later on.'

We strolled out into the brilliant sunshine and she said chattily, slipping her arm through mine, 'It's a small world, Susan. Stephen works in Hanover Square, and for eighteen months I worked round the corner at Claridge's, yet we never met. Now in London I could believe it if you'd had your car stolen, but down here, where nothing ever happens . . .'

'Stephen thinks the men who took it were joy-riding and that they'll abandon it when they get where they want to go.'

She nodded her head in agreement. 'I'm sure he's right. You must let me know what happens. Perhaps I can take you on a tour round on my day off.' She snapped her fingers. 'I'd put a little booklet that I thought might interest you on the reception desk, and I've come out without it.' She paused, making no effort to go back for it herself.

The inference was obvious, and I left them together, going back in the coolness of the foyer for the booklet. Feeling rather a gooseberry, I took my time and as I glanced through the window I saw my assumption had been correct. Christina had wanted to talk to Stephen alone. Her gaiety had left her and she was talking hurriedly, her face anxious. Uncomfortably I strolled back down the wooden steps and across to the car. Christina turned, smiling once more.

'Yes, that's the right book. It has a whole list of places that most tourists miss. Have a look through and tell me what you think. I do hope you hear good news when you get back.'

She stood, smiling and waving, as we took the Niedernhall road once more.

After a little while, Stephen said, 'As was no doubt obvious, Christina wanted to speak to me alone.' He paused, changing gear and sweeping round the bend of the road. 'She says she spoke to her father about the Herr Cliburn we mentioned, and he tells her there is no one of that name living in Niedernhall that he knows of. She also said,' he added impassively, 'that her father knows everyone in the district and couldn't possibly be mistaken.'

Chapter Three

I sat silently for a while, gazing unseeingly at the vineyards and fruit trees that sped past. I should have gone straight to the police myself - it was what any sensible person would have done – not leave it to a complete stranger to report. Turning to Stephen I said with more confidence than I felt, 'I'm sure Christina's father can't know *everyone* in Niedernhall.'

He made no effort to banish my doubts.

'Can he?' I asked tentatively.

'That, Susan, is what we're going to find out. I'm beginning to think Mr Cliburn was just a little too good to be true.'

There was no answer to that, and I stared moodily at the shining surface of the nearby river, its banks thick with celandines and buttercups. A kingfisher, the sun glinting on its bright blue and emerald plumage, swooped and dived, but I was scarcely aware of it. Even Stephen's presence did nothing to dispel my growing anxiety.

There was a stiff breeze blowing and I pushed my hair out of my eyes and opened my shoulder-bag, reaching for my headsquare. It wasn't there. I searched through the bag hastily, then felt in my pockets.

'What's the matter?'

'My scarf. I must have left it at Ohringen.'

'Do you want to go back for it?'

'No. I'm more worried about the car at the moment.'

'Don't worry. I'll see to it you're not left without transport,' said Stephen capably, 'and I'll bring your scarf along next time I see you. What is it like?'

'Scarlet silk. You can't mistake it. Oh goodness, are we forced to drive this fast?' I asked nervously, as the passing trees merged into a green blur. Stephen obligingly slowed down. We rounded the next bend at a more leisurely fifty miles an hour and he began to tell me of his visit to Wies.

'It really is incredible, Susan. Quite isolated. You walk through dark forest then suddenly emerge in green meadows and in the middle is the church. Very unobtrusive and ordinary looking. But inside it's fantastic. Baroque gone mad. You must see it before you leave.'

'Is there a shrine?'

'Oh yes, that's the reason the church was built. Way back in the early seventeen hundreds a couple of friars made a wooden statue of the Saviour out of fragments of saints' figures. Apparently it was carried round on Good Friday but aroused the faithful to such a degree that it was put away owing to its "ghastly and frightening" expression. A peasant's wife eventually took it and installed it in her farm at Wies, and claimed that, while praying in front of it, she had seen tears on the face. This so-called miracle was the beginning of a rapid rise of pilgrims. By the seventeen forties it was quite famous and lots of people came. The original church at Wies was too small to hold them all and so the present church was built. It really is worth seeing, though I can't promise any tears.'

'Sounds interesting. Providing I have a car I'll do as you suggest and pay it a visit.'

Ahead of us Niedernhall's church spire pierced the skyline and the afternoon sun shone hotly down on the steep roofs of the surrounding houses, gilding them a rich, deep red. Minutes later we were sliding over the bridge, past the watch-tower and into the main street.

'Whereabouts are you staying?'

'Right at the far end of the village. Oh, do be careful, Stephen! We nearly ran over a hen then.'

With a flurry of indignant feathers and a screech of protest the hen headed for the safety of the verge, and we continued through the narrow streets with Stephen giving every feathered jay-walker a toot on his horn.

'It's the house on the left. The one with all the flowers outside, just before the horses.'

A few yards beyond Frau Schmidt's brightly-painted front door stood two cart-horses harnessed to a high-sided cart loaded with wine casks. They looked very festive, with red poppies tucked gaily over each ear and large collars studded with polished brass around their necks. They hardly stirred their tails as Stephen drew up immediately in front of them.

Scarcely waiting for the car to come to a halt, I was out and running through the narrow, dark passage that led from the street to Frau Schmidt's living quarters.

'Frau Schmidt, has anyone . . . '

'So, you are back so soon,' she said to me with a welcoming smile. 'Vot was the matter, the day it is lovely.'

'No, it isn't lovely at all. Someone stole my car.'

'Pardon. I not understand.'

She rose from her chair and reached for a bottle of schnapps, pouring out a glass for herself and handing me another.

'Now, dat is not right.'

It was obvious that Gunther Cliburn had not been here and that my car had not been returned. I sat down wearily, and said with a descriptive wave of the hand, 'My car, *wagen*, gone, poof.'

'Gone. Gone vere? Vat is this gone?'

'It's been stolen,' I groaned. 'What on earth am I going to do?'

She crossed the room, taking my hand in hers uncomprehendingly.

'Nein, nein, Susan, meine Liebe.'

I managed a smile. 'Please don't get upset. I must go now. The sooner I see the police the better.'

'Polizei?' The lines of worry on her face deepened.

'I'll explain later, Frau Schmidt. I must go now.'

With less haste than I had entered, I went back to the waiting car. Stephen looked up expectantly and I shook my head.

'He hasn't been.'

Dejectedly I opened the door and sank into the seat.

20

Stephen looked at his watch, his lips set in a firm line.

'It's ten to three, Susan. We'll give him until three, then I'll take you to the police station.'

'It's what I should have done in the first place. It seemed so easy, though, when he said he'd handle it all.'

'Put not your trust . . . ' began Stephen. Then, realizing that I was really worried, his voice softened. 'Hey, not so much of the high drama. We'll get the whole thing sorted out. Stop worrying.'

I flushed slightly. 'You must think me an awful fool.'

'Why? For having your car stolen? Don't talk rubbish. Mind you,' he added, 'it doesn't happen to everyone.'

I gave a rueful laugh. 'It's the story of my life. Losing things. I hardly ever came home from school with everything I started out with. You name it and I'd lost it. But not even I thought I'd manage to lose a car.'

'You didn't,' he corrected mildly. 'It was stolen.'

'Yes, it was, wasn't it?' I replied with a bit more spirit. 'And I jolly well mean to get it back.'

'That's more like it.' He leaned back comfortably in his seat. 'You're not a Londoner, are you?'

'Good heavens, no. All I know of London are the railway stations and air terminals. I've never spent more than a night there. I come from a small village in the Dales. Nutwood is the original backwater to end all backwaters.'

'But you like it?'

I paused reflectively. 'I suppose I do. I wouldn't pine if I were away from it, but you can't live all your life in one place and not become attached to it, can you?'

'Thinking of some places, yes,' said Stephen with a grin. 'Are there many of you?'

'I beg your pardon?'

'Brothers and sisters, have you many?'

'No. Just Grandma.'

He raised an eyebrow enquiringly.

'My father left us for pastures new several years ago. Mother died shortly afterwards and I went to live with

21

Grandma and Great Aunt Sophie. The house is huge. It was built in the days when families really were families and there were servants to be accommodated as well. Now we just live in a few rooms on the ground floor. All the rest is locked up and empty.'

Stephen groaned. 'A place like that in London would be worth a fortune – think of the flats it could be turned into.'

'Not while Grandma's alive,' I said, laughing. 'The very thought would have her on the warpath. She's what is known as a formidable old lady.'

'And Great Aunt Sophie? Tell me about her.'

'There isn't really anything to say about Aunt Sophie. She's a spinster and has always lived with Grandma. I'm afraid she's rather put upon. Grandma takes it for granted that Aunt Sophie is there to do all her running about and treats her as an unpaid maid.'

'Rough on Aunt Sophie.'

'Not really. I know it sounds unkind, but she's a natural-born doormat. She would be utterly miserable if she couldn't be doing things for others. She adores Grandma, and to be fair, her life would have been pretty bleak if it hadn't been for Grandma taking her in. The arrangement is ideal. Grandma has someone to boss around, and Aunt Sophie has someone to boss her, so they're both happy.'

'And you? Are you happy?'

'Me? Yes, I suppose so. I haven't given it much thought.'

'No possessive boy-friend on the scene?'

'No boy-friend, let alone possessive,' I said, feeling suddenly shy.

'And what do you do in this matriarchal society?'

'Oh, I escape from it sometimes. I work in the village library, though I must admit men are in pretty short supply there as well.' I giggled. 'Grandma was horrified when I told her Miss Brookes had asked if I would assist her there.'

'What on earth for?' asked Stephen. 'I would have thought the village library the ultimate in respectability.'

'Ah, but you don't know Grandma. She mistrusts men and

is never happy if she thinks I may become what she calls a 'prey' to them.'

'In the local library!' exclaimed Stephen disbelievingly.

'I'll have you know that Grandma regards the library as a cross between the Playboy Club and an army barracks.'

He burst out laughing. 'Good grief! How did you manage to escape as far as the Continent unaccompanied?'

'It wasn't easy!' Then: 'She isn't quite so bad now. I've worked at the library for five years and during that time she's gradually reconciled herself to all sorts of things that would once have been taboo.'

Just then two men, wearing large leather aprons, emerged from the doorway next to Frau Schmidt's. They disappeared behind the cart, and then returned, rolling a barrel on to the ground and into the depths of the building's cellars. I watched silently, my thoughts centred once more on my missing car. When a second barrel had rolled, with a great deal of noise, into the shop, the men jumped up behind the patiently waiting horses and with a light touch of the reins the cart rolled out into the middle of the road, made a detour round our stationary vehicle, and clattered away over the cobbled stones.

I sat and stared in front of me disbelievingly. There, the wheels thick with mud, looking the dearest sight in all the world, was my old Morris. I grabbed hold of Stephen's arm excitedly.

'Look, Stephen! It's there! That's it. My car. Right in front of us!'

I scrambled out hastily, sped towards the car, and ran my hands thankfully over the battered bodywork. The door was open and the keys were in the glove compartment. A large white envelope was propped on the steering wheel, with Fraulein Carter written across the front in a bold, heavy hand. The message was brief and to the point. Gunther Cliburn had been called away and had been unable to wait for my return. He would pick me up at eight o'clock.

'Isn't it marvellous!' I exclaimed joyfully. 'I'd given up all hope of seeing it again. Apart from the dirt it doesn't even look damaged.'

Stephen, examining it closely, agreed.

I patted the faded leather seats. 'You were right all along about it being taken for a joy-ride.'

Stephen, hands in his pockets, surveyed it thoughtfully. I laughed. 'You're looking more worried now I've got it back than you were when it was missing.'

'Sorry.' The frown disappeared but he still looked puzzled. 'Just seems a little odd, don't you think?'

'Odd? Nothing of the sort. It seems absolutely marvellous.'

Whatever it was that Stephen found odd about the car's return I dismissed with a careless wave of the hand.

'I refuse point blank to worry about the affair any more. It's back, that's all that matters to me. How and where it's been I don't even want to know.'

'What a typical display of feminine logic. Well, whatever the whys and wherefores it calls for a celebration. How about coming back with me to Ohringen for dinner this evening?'

'I'd have loved to, Stephen, only . . . ' I tapped the note in my hand. 'Gunther Cliburn says he's picking me up at eight. I'd better see him – hadn't I? – to thank him for what he's done.'

'We've heaps of time till then, it's only just gone three. How about a drive? And a bottle of wine to celebrate the return of your car?'

I let him take my hand, and strolled with him down the sun-dappled street to buy the wine.

Chapter Four

Half an hour later we were skimming along the tree-lined road that skirted the banks of the Neckar.

'I know a perfect spot. That is, if you don't mind a walk,' Stephen said, as all traces of Niedernhall disappeared in the distance.

'A walk would be nice, but don't forget I have to be back by eight.'

'Have no fear.' He grinned. 'Though all's fair in love and war.'

I let that pass and said, 'How long a walk is it to your spot?'

'Oh, not far. About a half a mile, but it's all cross country.'

'I see, and what's so special about the view when we get there?'

'Nothing. Not a single thing.'

I raised my eyebrow. So why . . . '

He grinned. 'You're a nosey little girl, Susan Carter. Grandma ever tell you that?'

'Not in so many words.'

'Well, I'm not going to put you out of your misery. You'll have to wait and see why I think our destination is so special. In fact you won't have long to wait. This is where we start to foot it.'

He drove the car off the road and halted under the leafy tentacles of a willow tree. There was a slight breeze blowing and I slipped my arms into the sleeves of my cardigan before picking up the paper carrier that held our wine.

'Here, let me take that.' He took the carrier away from me, imprisoning my now free right hand firmly in his.

Ahead of us were meadows thick with wild flowers and the ground gradually became steeper and steeper until we entered the leafy dimness of the woods. We fell silent as, hand in hand, we picked our way between the tree-trunks, the air smelling sweetly of damp earth and moss.

'Do you believe they have souls?' asked Stephen suddenly.

'Trees? Oh yes, and that they cry when being felled.' I pulled my cardigan closer round my shoulders. 'No wonder ancient peoples met to worship in woods. The whole atmosphere is spirit-laden.'

'Talking of which,' said Stephen, 'look down there.'

I pushed the low-hanging branch in front of me to one side and gasped.

At our feet the ground shelved steeply away, forming a hollow. Here there were no trees and the sun shone down brightly on the carpet of grass and flowers. In the cup of the hollow were the derelict and deserted ruins of a tiny church. Weeds and moss had grown over the scattered stones, but one wall still stood, its arched window half submerged by brambles and thickets.

'Oh Stephen, it's beautiful. How ever did you find it?'

'Quite by accident. I shouldn't think there are many people aware of its existence. Even Christina's father looked blank when I told him about it. Come on, let's go down. Be careful though, it's very steep.'

For the second time that day I scrambled down an overgrown hillside, though this time, with Stephen's arm for support, the experience was more pleasant. We reached the ruins in their little oasis of pasture. The dark green pines and the steep banks that enclosed us were gloomy and forbidding, but amid the riotous jungle of shrubs and creepers growing round the twisted, crumbling stones, all was light and sunshine.

Taking the one remaining wall as a guide, we traced out on the springy turf where the others had once stood; then, my back resting upon all that was left of a roughly hewn pillar, I sprinkled a few drops of wine on the ground in a libation for the Gods.

'Heathen,' said Stephen, taking the bottle from me and

raising it to his lips.

'Appropriate though. It must have been a place of worship long before this Christian church was built.'

'I dare say you're right,' he said agreeably. 'They must have been a very stalwart congregation to brave the woods and that steep descent every time they came though.'

'I expect they came from a different direction.' I looked round searchingly at the enclosing hills. 'See, over there, it looks as if there could be a narrow gully. The church is probably quite accessible.'

Stephen screwed up his eyes against the sun.

'Yes, I think you're right. Let's go and look.'

'Not me,' I said firmly, leaning my head on the cool stone. 'I've done all the climbing I'm going to do for one day.'

'Lazybones.' Stephen sprang to his feet. 'I'm going for a wander round. Shan't be long.'

It was very still. I was drifting pleasantly off to sleep when something whistled close to my ear, ricocheting off the rock beside me. Involuntarily I shrank away. Then another bullet sang through the air, glancing off the rock some inches to my left. This time I screamed, and kept on screaming.

Stephen hurtled out of the undergrowth, racing across the glade towards me. The firing stopped and my knees gave way.

'What the hell happened? Are you all right?' He grasped my shoulders roughly, face white. 'For God's sake, what happened?'

I steadied my breathing and managed a weak smile. 'Some fool out shooting. He couldn't have seen me down here and the shots landed inches away.' I blew my nose shakily. 'I must have scared him to death when I started screaming.'

'You must have scared *him*!' Stephen expostulated angrily. 'Where did the bullets come from?'

I pointed with a still trembling hand to the trees skirting the crest of the steep bank we had just scrambled down.

'Stay there.'

He raced over the glade and rapidly climbed the ridge, then the light blue of his shirt disappeared among the ferns and

27

dark foliage, and the afternoon was as still, as quiet, as before.

My fear had turned to anger and I hoped Stephen caught up with whoever it was. Of all the stupid, thoughtless things to do! I lit a cigarette, wondering what poor, innocent animal the gunman had been aiming at.

A few minutes later I caught a glimpse of Stephen through the trees, then a minute later he reached the top of the ridge. He waved his hands negatively. I waved back to show I understood, then watched as he sprang agilely down the slope and over the rough scree.

'No luck, Susan. The bastard got away.'

'What would he have been hunting, Stephen? It's not the open season for anything, is it?'

'Not a clue. I'd have thought the only thing he would get here would be rabbits — or the occasional tourist.'

I laughed. 'He nearly did that all right. I've never been so scared in all my life. Between you and me I'll be very glad when today is over.'

'I don't blame you. Is life as eventful in Nutwood?'

'No, thank goodness.' I frowned. 'I think that man must have been a poacher.'

'What makes you say that?'

'Well, if it was legal to hunt here, he wouldn't be using a silencer, would he?'

'I wouldn't have thought so, but then I wouldn't have thought anyone would be shooting so haphazardly in the first place. Would you prefer it if we went home?'

'I think so. It's getting late and I've Gunther Cliburn to see yet.'

'Ah yes, mustn't make you late for your date,' he said lightly. 'And don't forget to ask Herr Cliburn where the police picked up your car and if they intend apprehending the men who stole it. They'll have had to tow the other one away by now and I imagine they'll already have traced the name and address of the owner. I'd be very interested to know how your car was retrieved so speedily.'

'I'll try not to be so bowled over by Herr Cliburn's charm

28

that I forget to ask for all the details,' I said, as we began to climb the bank. 'After all, I'm just as interested as you are.'

At that moment the earth beneath my feet fell away suddenly and I slithered ungainly downwards.

'You're not a very good mountaineer, are you?'

'I'm not *any* sort of mountaineer,' I replied darkly, grasping Stephen's hand and hauling myself up.

'Grandma should have sent you to the Guides – it would have proved a useful experience.'

'Going by the events of today, so would the Territorials!'

Laughing and breathless we reached the top, and walked back through the trees to the waiting car.

'How about visiting Wies with me tomorrow?' Stephen asked, as he backed the car on to the road.

'That would be lovely. Are you sure you want to? I mean, if you've seen it already you may not want to see it again.'

'Susan,' he said with exaggerated patience, 'if I hadn't wanted to go myself I wouldn't have suggested it to you. Now, are you coming?'

'Yes, please,' I said meekly. 'I'll bring the food and wine.'

'Good girl. And wear some flat shoes, those are ridiculous.'

I glanced down at my muddied sandals. Considering the treatment I had subjected them to, they had stood up to it rather well, but the white leather was stained green with the grass and leaves, and the heels were caked with dry mud.

'I will, but I hope you're not contemplating another day like today. If you are, I'll stay at home.'

'Relax. Tomorrow will be a leisurely day sightseeing. No car thieves, no trigger-happy marksmen.'

I laughed. 'You've talked me into it. What time are we setting off?'

'I'll pick you up between seven and seven-thirty. It's quite a way.'

'You realize that is the crack of dawn for me when I'm on holiday?'

'You won't have to stay out late tonight then, will you?'

'That,' I said, 'is my affair.'

29

'Till tomorrow then.' He drew up outside Frau Schmidt's whitewashed cottage. 'And be a good girl. Keep out of trouble.'

Lightheartedly I watched as he turned round, scattering hens and pigeons to the right and left, then with a wave raced down the narrow street. I stood in the doorway until he had disappeared over the bridge, then in a much happier frame of mind, went indoors.

Frau Schmidt was waiting for me, her face anxious. 'The *Polizei*, have you go?'

I gave her ample figure a hug. 'Everything is all right. My car is back. Look.' I pointed through the tiny window to my Morris.

She spread out her hands. 'Vat 'appened? Vat is wrong?'

Slowly I repeated. 'My car, my automobile, was stolen, taken, gone. Now it is back.'

'No *Polizei*?'

'No *Polizei*, Frau Schmidt. Everything is fine. In fact, things couldn't be better.'

She laughed then, still not understanding. '*Gut, gut*,' she said.

I went upstairs for a badly needed wash and change of clothes.

The late afternoon sun streamed through the open window on to the polished wood floor, the bare white walls reflecting the light. I closed the shutters, then slowly and wearily took off my clothes, laying them neatly on the bed. By the time I had washed all over in cold water from the ewer and rubbed myself dry with the rough towel, I felt completely revived. I wondered if Gunther Cliburn would simply tell me the details regarding my car's return, or if he would also be taking me out, and if so, where.

After some hesitation I chose a navy dress that flared gently from the hips, twisted my hair into a chignon and sprayed perfume on my wrists and throat. A glance at my watch showed that it was still only six o'clock.

Throwing a jacket round my shoulders I went downstairs

for a chat with Frau Schmidt, but as there was no sign of her I strolled out into the back yard to see if she was feeding the rabbits. It was deserted save for the furry inmates in their cages. Bending down, I stroked a twitching nose, trying hard not to think of its eventual fate in Frau Schmidt's cooking pot, then walked back through the house and out into the street.

In the short time it had taken me to dress, the sun had disappeared behind heavy clouds, and the breeze, too, had died down. There was the breathless, oppressive feeling which presages a storm.

I left the main street and wandered aimlessly through the unpaved alleyways, thinking about Stephen and our day out tomorrow. There weren't many people about. They were either having tea, or had no wish to risk a drenching when the storm broke. I pulled my jacket closer round my shoulders, looking at the threatening sky. I quickened my pace and began to make my way back. Five minutes later I stood hopelessly lost amongst the hotch-potch of barns and cottages.

I gazed despairingly up the narrow passageway I found myself in, but there was nothing to indicate the whereabouts of the main street. I looked back the way I had come, but it was no use. I had lost all sense of direction. There was nothing but the backs of the small cottages.

Picking my way carefully over the hay and débris strewn on the ground, I continued to the intersection at the top. This alleyway looked as unpromising as the previous one and I increased my pace. Despite the approaching storm there was still some daylight, but it would not last long, and I shuddered at the thought of wandering for hours in the maze of tortuous streets.

I approached the next corner briskly and, turning it, breathed a sigh of relief.

The street was cobbled and had a narrow pavement, and crossing it at the far end I could see a small section of concrete indicating the main street. As I drew nearer, I recognized the door of a wine bar; a few seconds later, the door opened and a thick-set figure, vaguely familiar, hurried out, a bottle tucked securely under one arm. I shooed a few too friendly hens out of the way and then stopped short.

That was one of the men who had stolen my car! The clothes were different, but there was no doubt about that moustache. I broke into a run after him, but by the time I had reached the main street he was nowhere to be seen. There were only a couple of women, their shawls clutched tightly beneath their chins.

I took a deep breath and as I ran along the street I hastily scanned each side street, but there was not a sign of him. I ran past Frau Schmidt's and towards the bridge, but it was a waste of time. The bird had flown. Weakly I leaned against the ivy-covered stone of the village walls, my heart thumping painfully.

For the first time I became aware that the storm had broken at last and rain was falling fast. In another few minutes I would be soaked. I pulled myself upright and began to trudge back to my lodgings. As I did so I heard a car start up some distance away. It slowed down as it turned into the street, then speeded past me for the watch-tower. There was no mistaking the man at the wheel.

I watched helplessly as the distance between us increased, then the car slowed down at an obstruction in the road. I ran towards my parked Morris and a few minutes after he disappeared over the bridge, I followed.

It was pure impulse. If I'd had time to think I don't suppose I would have acted so hastily, but I couldn't help feeling that, if ever anyone was owed an explanation, I was.

Burning with righteous indignation, I swept out of the village, foot pressed hard down on the accelerator. There was no other traffic about and I had no difficulty following him, although he was some way ahead.

About two miles outside the village he turned right on to a little used country lane, then, after a mile or so, turned left, disappearing from view.

When I drew up some minutes later I could see nothing

more than a roughly beaten track leading off the lane into the woods, but the heavy indentations of tyre marks in the churned earth showed where he had been.

I wasn't so keen on following him that I was going to risk embedding the car in what would, very shortly, be a sea of mud. The rough track ran across open country for fifty yards or so, then disappeared as the ground rose steeply into woodland, appearing again beyond the thick belt of trees, leading finally to a large, stone-built farmhouse standing in windswept isolation on the hillside. As I looked, the car I had been following crawled from the pines and continued on its way to the house. It seemed I had hunted my quarry to earth.

I felt pleased with myself. Perhaps the police already knew his identity and where he lived. Perhaps there was a rational explanation for his behaviour. No doubt Gunther would tell me when I saw him. But if they *didn't* know who he was and where he lived, I'd be only too happy to pass on the information.

I was about to reverse when the glint of something metallic in the woods caught my eye. The heavy clouds had darkened the evening prematurely and it was difficult to tell, but I was pretty certain it was a car parked under cover of the trees. A courting couple probably, and yet . . . I left the car and set off on foot up the muddy track. After a few yards I left it, heading diagonally in a short cut across the fields.

It wasn't exactly a pleasant country ramble. The incline was steeper than it had looked and the rain was heavy, but when I entered the dimness of the woods and saw clearly what it was parked there, I judged my journey had been worthwhile.

The car was Stephen's.

Chapter Five

I stared at it in perplexity. Almost absent-mindedly I tried the car door. To my surprise it opened. Even more surprising, his keys were in the ignition. I stared round at the dripping trees but there was no sign of Stephen. Mystified, I sat in the driver's seat and waited. In a deluge like this he surely wouldn't be long, but the minutes ticked by and he didn't appear.

I rummaged in the glove compartment, gratefully finding a packet of cigarettes and eyed the water-logged ground apprehensively. If Stephen didn't hurry the car would be bogged down until the ground dried out. I glanced at my watch. Seven-thirty and I had to meet Gunther at eight.

Shivering, I stubbed out the cigarette and lit another. There was a distant rumble of thunder and the rain was falling more heavily. I slipped the packet of cigarettes back into the glove compartment and reluctantly opened the door. If I stayed much longer I was going to find myself marooned. My feet sank in the soft earth, mud oozing squelchily into my shoes. I floundered to the edge of the woods on to the slightly firmer ground and paused to look back.

Further up the hill, in front of the farmhouse, were the blurred figures of two men. The rain dripped uncomfortably down my neck and I hurried over the slippery grass towards my car. Once in it, I eased off my sodden jacket and took my binoculars out of my bag. I wound the window down and, wiping raindrops from my eyes, focused intently. The figures were a long way off and the rain made it almost impossible to be sure, but one looked very much like Stephen and the other was the man I had been following, one of the men who had taken my car.

The rain drummed rhythmically down on the roof, running in tiny rivulets and eddies down the windows and over the bonnet. It was a terrible night. Not fit for a dog to be out in. Yet out there in that hostile countryside, not very far away from me, was Stephen Maitland. Whatever his reasons for being there, surely now that the storm had broken with such vengeance, he would soon head back for the safety of the tarmacked road? Unless it was his intention to shelter in the farmhouse.

I sat and watched for a movement in the dwindling light, but in vain. There was no sound of a car engine being started up in the woods. No headlights. Only the incessant lashing of the rain.

I would gain nothing by sitting at the roadside all night, that much was obvious. Besides, I had a date. Stephen Maitland and his nocturnal wanderings could wait until tomorrow. If he wanted to catch pneumonia it was his affair. Subdued and puzzled, I drove slowly back to Niedernhall, peering with difficulty through the streaming windscreen.

Gunther was already parked outside Frau Schmidt's when I arrived. I pulled up in front of him and then, as he opened his door for me, I picked up my jacket and made a quick dash through the rain from one car to the other, sinking gratefully into the upholstered seat. Warm air blew welcomingly round my frozen legs. It was no wonder the thieves had dumped my draughty old Morris so speedily.

'I was beginning to think you had drowned somewhere,' he said, taking my jacket. Then, disbelievingly, as he felt it: 'Where *have* you been, Susan? Swimming?'

'Walking.'

'My God! In this?' He waved a hand descriptively at the filthy night outside the oasis of warmth and comfort. 'The English are the strangest race. You will need something to warm you. A brandy perhaps?'

'A brandy would be lovely,' I said, teeth chattering.

'Good. I'm glad to see you are not teetotal. I had an uncle who said all English women were teetotal and that they loved only cats. Your walking about in the middle of a thunderstorm would have surprised him not in the slightest.' Then, more to himself: 'I think perhaps with the brandy, a meal. Yes, definitely a meal.'

The large car slid over the bridge and into the night. He turned, seeming suddenly larger and more forceful in the intimacy of the darkened car.

'I am sorry I could not be there to hand your car back to you, Susan.'

'That's all right. I'm very grateful to you for all the trouble you have gone to as it is. Where did they find it?'

'As to that, I am not quite sure.' He shrugged. 'Somewhere in the vicinity. The other car, too, was stolen. Though its owner was not so lucky. Obviously the men wanted to go somewhere in a hurry and took what was available.'

He changed gear smoothly and the needle on the speedometer swung beyond seventy.

'You have been lucky, I think. You will hear no more about the matter.'

'What? No statement, no forms to fill in?'

'To spoil your holiday? But certainly not.'

'Did they catch the thieves with the car?'

'Heavens, Susan, it is we who are supposed to be a thorough race. Your car is back, you have no more problems. Let us enjoy ourselves. No doubt your gentlemen friends will reap their reward.'

I hesitated, tempted to tell Gunther that I had seen and followed one of my gentlemen friends not ten minutes ago, but I would have to mention Stephen's presence, and I didn't want to spend the evening speculating about him with Gunther.

The thunder and lightning were in the far distance and the rain only a light drizzle when we finally drew up before a large hotel. I was painfully aware of my muddy shoes and rain-spattered stockings, but Gunther appeared not to care. With his hand lightly under my arm he led me inside.

A corner table and a bottle of wine appeared in quick

succession. As I enjoyed the smoked salmon and then the beautifully cooked lamb that followed, coated in an exquisite sauce, all thoughts of Stephen faded into the background. I had nothing more important to think about than whether to choose the asparagus in butter or the broccoli. It was Gunther who broke this carefree idyll. Spearing a forkful of the tiny button mushrooms, he said, 'I nearly forgot, Susan. I have a message for you.'

I looked up, surprised.

'Frau Schmidt informs me that Mr Maitland called, saying he will be a little late in the morning'.

I coloured slightly. 'Oh?'

'Yes. Apparently he has gone to Koblenz tonight. It is a long drive and he doesn't expect to be back until the early hours of the morning.'

'I see,' I said slowly, not seeing at all. 'Gunther – '

'Why,' Gunther continued, pouring out more wine, 'a late night should entail him being late in the morning, I do not know. Perhaps – ' he smiled – 'perhaps he is not used to them.'

I smiled back over my glass, deciding that my loyalty lay with Stephen. It may have been the wine, but I felt more resentful at his behaviour than bewildered. Koblenz indeed! I didn't like being lied to, and I was sure that any delay in the morning would be due to the fact that Mr Maitland's car was irretrievably bogged down in a field just outside Niedernhall.

Gunther dismissed the subject of Stephen and concentrated on boosting my ego. After the meal there was dancing on the tiny dance-floor adjoining the dining-room. Three or four other couples moved slowly round us, lulled by the wine and music into contented silence, or talking in soft undertones.

'It's a great pity, Susan,' Gunther said, his lips brushing the hair above my ear, 'that you are leaving so soon.'

'I have another week yet.' I tried to keep out of my voice any inference as to what could happen in a week. I didn't want to give Gunther encouragement. He was doing very well without any. The small band played a few more bars.

'That is good.' His hand increased its pressure on mine. Silently we revolved round the dimly-lit floor once more, then returned to our table and more drinks.

'I'll pick you up at seven tomorrow night, Susan.'

Uncomfortably I said, 'I'm sorry, I'm afraid I . . . '

He waved my protestations aside. 'Your Mr Maitland? Surely he is not going to command your company all day long? I will come for you at seven. I think you will be back by then. Would you like another drink?'

I shook my head.

'A coffee?'

'Lovely.'

I leaned back in my chair, enjoying the feeling of well-being induced by the alcohol and good food. The coffee, when it came, was delicious. Hot and strong and served with fresh cream. Everything had been perfect.

As I put my drained cup down, I said, 'It was a beautiful meal, Gunther. Thank you.'

'The pleasure was mine. Would you like to dance again? They're playing your tune.'

I had the grace to blush as he led me, hand held firmly in his, on to the dance-floor to the soft strains of 'Sweet and Lovely'.

We stayed another hour before we left. The air outside was clear and fresh after the storm, and the moon rode high and bright in the sky above us as we drove back in silence to Niedernhall.

The village was in complete darkness as the big car eased its way through the winding streets, drawing to a halt outside Frau Schmidt's. He slipped his arm along the back of the seat behind me and pulled me to him. His mouth was harder than I had expected and more demanding. It was no polite good night kiss. I tried to think of something to say but couldn't find the words. I pushed him away, fumbling unnecessarily with my handbag. The tension in the car was electric, and then he gave a light laugh and opened the car door.

'Good night, Cinderella. Perhaps tomorrow will be even

more enjoyable.'

I smiled. 'Good night, Gunther, and thank you again for a lovely evening.'

He remained in the car as I let myself into the darkened house and climbed the steeply polished stairs. Then I heard the car turn round in the narrow street and roar off over the bridge.

As I got ready for bed, I wondered idly just where Gunther lived. But I was too tired to dwell overlong on the subject. I climbed into bed, and snuggled down under the voluminous eiderdown. Perhaps it was as well Stephen was going to be late in the morning, was my last thought as I fell to sleep.

Stephen Maitland was not only late the next morning, he didn't arrive at all! Furiously angry at such behaviour I paced the wooden floor of my room. It was a beautiful day. The sun streamed through the open window and puffs of white cloud drifted enticingly across the blue sky, and here I was, stuck in the house, awaiting collection like a parcel. By lunchtime I ran out of patience. I renewed my lipstick, collected my bag and binoculars and made my way downstairs to the car. I sat behind the wheel indecisively. Should I? Shouldn't I?

It would only take five minutes and the curiosity would kill me if I didn't. I retraced my route of the previous evening. I'm not sure if I had hoped to find Stephen's car still there or not. As it was, the woods were empty. The ground was still soft and muddy from the storm of the previous night and I didn't walk right up into the trees, but the place where Stephen's car had been parked was now deserted. At least if he had still been marooned there, it would have explained his non-arrival. What other explanation could there be? It was foolish but I felt sure Stephen would not have let me down. More foolish still, I told myself, was the fact that I should let it bother me, even if he had. With growing irritation I went back to the village.

It seemed a shame to waste such a glorious day pottering negatively backwards and forwards, but I couldn't settle to

39

making alternative plans. There was still no sign of his car in the street. Listlessly I went back to the house and sat on the bed, trying to minimize the crushing disappointment I felt as I smoked one cigarette after another.

By late he surely couldn't have meant this late. It was nearly one o'clock. Perhaps Gunther had mistaken the message. With a faint glimmer of hope I hurried downstairs to see Frau Schmidt, but her little living-room was empty. I would have to do something. I couldn't spend the rest of the day waiting. I had been stood up and that was that. Better face the truth and stop dreaming. Picking up a newspaper that was lying on the table, I went across the road to the crowded coffee-shop and sat, half ashamed of myself, at a window-table giving a clear view of the street.

Idly I flicked through the pages, turning to the society page as I sipped my hot coffee. The usual faces in the usual places stared back.

The street outside was full of busy housewives, baskets over their arms, going to or coming from market. No white Sprite drew up outside Frau Schmidt's and no dark head scanned the village street looking for me.

Angrily I turned to the front page. Across it was splashed a lurid account of the assassination of Herr Heinrich Ahlers, one of Germany's leading cabinet ministers. There were large photographs of the minister speaking at a public rally in Bonn. I couldn't read the accompanying newsprint and all I knew about the minister was that he was a liberal, pro-British, and had been active in bringing to justice many Nazi war criminals. There was a photograph of his bloodstained body spread-eagled across the speaker's platform. Lower down was a picture of his wife, taken at a recent reception. She was large and blonde and cheerful and I felt sorry for her. I pushed the cup of coffee away and spread the paper on the table.

I was in the act of turning the page when I noticed the photograph of the car. Despite the foreign background of beach and sea, it looked vaguely familiar. It was familiar!

40

It was the same car the thieves had crashed before taking mine. I stared at the number plate in horrified fascination, my mind refusing to take in the awful fact. But it was the same. I was sure it was the same. Frantically I tried to decipher the words below it but without success. I rose, taking the paper over to the elderly man serving behind the counter.

'Excuse me. Do you speak English?'

'A little, Fraulein,' he said courteously, laying down the knife with which he was buttering slices of rye bread. I pointed to the newspaper article and then to the photograph of the car.

'Could you tell me how this car is connected with Herr Ahlers' death?'

He shook his head, pursing his lips as he did so. 'The assassins, they take.'

'They what! But that's impossible! It's . . . '

He shrugged his shoulders, wiping his hands on the large apron round his waist. 'Is possible, Fraulein. The car belong to . . . a – ' He struggled to find the word. Then with a triumphant rush . . . 'An official, not important, you understand. He did not report it missing till long after. The police, they have not found it, so is possible the killer took it. Who knows?'

I knew. With sickening clarity I remembered their panic. The angry words that passed between them after they had crashed. The frantic looking-back along the road. Their desperate dash to my Morris. The men who had stolen my car had murdered Heinrich Ahlers.

Slowly I went back to my seat and spread the paper once more on the table in front of me. It didn't make sense. It didn't make any sense at all.

If the whole country was looking for them, how come the police hadn't descended on me like vultures when Gunther had reported the crash and subsequent theft of my car? Mechanically I lifted the cup and took a sip of coffee. My car must have been abandoned locally. Perhaps it had been towed in, left in a restricted area, so that when Gunther reported the loss it was there. And, of course, until they went to the scene of the crash they wouldn't realize the car was the one every police force in the country was looking for. I hadn't thought to take its registration number, and I was pretty sure Gunther hadn't either. That must be it, and the men I saw . . .

I stared at the paper numbly. There were no pictures of the wanted men. Slowly it dawned on me that the police didn't know who they were or what they looked like. But I did. And I knew where they were hiding, or at least where one of them was hiding. And so did Stephen.

I closed my eyes, ridding my sight of the hideous picture of the dead man. Stephen had to be told. Now. Straightaway, and so had the police.

Clutching the paper, I went out into the street and the bright sunlight.

I was in the telephone kiosk before I realized that I didn't have Stephen's number. What was the guest-house called? I drummed my fingers on the directories but it was no use. I'd never noticed the name of it, and I didn't know Christina's surname. I scrabbled hastily through my bag for the card Gunther had given me bearing his telephone number, and dialled the number with shaking hands. It rang only once before he answered.

'Gunther, thank goodness you're in.' Then, unnecessarily: 'It's Susan.'

'Good morning, Susan. This is an unexpected pleasure. I thought you would be buried deep in the countryside with your fellow countryman by now.'

'Gunther. The men who took my car were the men who killed Heinrich Ahlers.'

'Were the men who did what? This line is bad, Susan. You will have to speak up a little.'

I said as calmly as I could, 'They killed Heinrich Ahlers. It's in all the papers. He was assassinated in Bonn yesterday, and the car the police suspect the killers left the city in, is the one my car thieves crashed.'

'Susan — ,' his voice was patient — 'the car may be the

42

same model, but it isn't possible that it's the same car.'

'But it *is*!' I insisted, feeling hysteria rising within me. 'The number plates are the same. I'm sure of it.'

There was a slight pause at the other end of the phone, then I heard the rustle of newspaper. His voice, when he spoke again, was brusque. 'Stay at Frau Schmidt's. I'm going straight to the police. And, Susan, don't worry. The men in question are probably in Austria by now, but at least you will be able to give a description of them. I'll see you shortly.'

'Gunther, just a minute! They're not in Austria. At least one of them isn't. There's a lot more I haven't told you yet. Yesterday evening, before I met you, I *saw* one of the men. In the village.'

He drew in his breath audibly. 'You must be imagining things,' he said finally.

'No, I'm not. It *was* him. I followed him.'

Now it was his turn to raise his voice. 'You did *what*?' he said. 'And didn't even tell me! For God's sake, Susan, why?'

I didn't attempt to answer that. I said, 'He went to a large farmhouse about two miles from the village.'

'Could you find it again?'

'Oh yes, I already have.'

'You've already *what*?'

'Well, you see, last night when I followed the man with the moustache, I saw Stephen's car nearby, and then I saw them talking, not very clearly because of the rain and it was getting dark, but I'm sure it was Stephen. He didn't arrive here this morning and so I thought the car must still be bogged down, so I went back to have a look. This was before I read the papers of course. I can't get in touch with Stephen to warn him because I can't remember the name of the guest-house where he's staying.'

'Susan, one thing at a time. You say Maitland's car was parked at this farmhouse last night?'

'Not actually at the farmhouse, but in the woods near the track leading to it.'

'And he was talking to this man?'

43

'Yes.' Then, as the expression in Gunther's voice penetrated my numbed brain, I said: 'But Stephen can't possibly know what's happened. It was just a coincidence.'

'All the same, Susan, if he comes before I get there, say nothing to him. Just in case.'

'Don't be ridiculous, Gunther. I must tell him as soon as possible for his own sake.'

'I am not being ridiculous,' Gunther said angrily. 'Your Mr Maitland left a message for you last night saying he was going to Koblenz, remember? Now either you are mistaken or he is lying. And if he's lying I'd like to know why. Another thing. He was practically driving with those two men, wasn't he? You told me yourself he wasn't very far behind them. Promise me you will say nothing to him until I've reported it all to the police.'

'All right, all right,' I said miserably. 'He won't be coming now anyway.'

'I know you think I am being over-cautious, Susan. But if he *is* involved, and he realizes how much you know . . . It just isn't worth the risk. I don't want any harm coming to you.'

Neither did I. The phone went dead and I put it slowly back on its cradle and stepped out into the street.

I didn't want to think about it any more, least of all of Stephen and where he fitted in. I would listen to what Gunther had to say when he came, see the police to give a description of the two men, then pack my bags and go further south.

Having come to this decision, I felt better and walked back to Frau Schmidt's.

Chapter Six

I lay down on my bed, and incredible though it seems, actually slept, or rather dozed, for it could only have been half an hour or so before I was awakened by loud knocking. Hastily I jumped up and ran across to the window. The car parked at the roadside was Stephen's.

I hurried downstairs. One thing was certain: if he had come, even though several hours late, to take me to Wies, he was out of luck. I couldn't leave the house till Gunther returned from the police station. Stephen stood in the open doorway, relaxed and smiling.

'Are you ready?' he said quite pleasantly and calmly.

'Am I ready?' I exclaimed unbelievingly, hardly able to believe my ears at his impertinence. 'I've been ready since seven-thirty this morning. What happened?'

'You got my message last night?'

'Yes, but . . . '

'Then you'll understand. I didn't get back from Koblenz until three in the morning, and as I'm a growing boy and need my sleep . . . '

'You mean you actually *went* to Koblenz last night?'

Dark brows lifted in surprise. 'But of course, – that's why I left a message. I knew I'd be late getting back and that I'd never make it over here by seven. I must have been mad to think I could anyway. Getting up early isn't one of my virtues.'

I stared at him, bewildered. 'What time did you leave?' I managed to ask.

'What's this – the inquisition?' he asked good-humouredly. 'I left immediately I dropped you off. Well, not quite immediately, but when I got back to Ohringen there was a

45

message for me requiring my presence in Koblenz. By rights I should have stayed the night, but as I had a date this morning with a particularly beautiful young woman, I spared no expense in getting back as quickly as possible. Now, are you ready?'

I simply couldn't stop staring at him. 'Did you drive there in that?' I said at last, nodding in the direction of the car.

'Yes. It may not be a Mercedes and what you're used to of late, but it's quite serviceable, and more than capable of making the journey to Koblenz and back in an evening. There's no need to be nervous. It won't suddenly die a death miles from anywhere, leaving us stranded.' He took a step towards me. 'What is it? Something bothering you? You don't look well.'

'I . . .'

'Come on.' He took my arm. 'Let's sit in the car. Clowning apart, Susan, I really am sorry about this morning. But it was unavoidable.'

He opened the car door for me and I sat obediently in the passenger seat.

'You don't look at all well this morning,' he repeated. 'What's wrong?'

'Nothing. It's just a headache.'

'Have you taken anything for it?'

'No, it isn't that bad. I must talk to you, Stephen. Something . . .'

'All in good time. First, I'm getting you something for that headache. You look like death.'

'No, Stephen. Please! . . .'

But he had already darted across the road into the chemist's. I took a deep breath, trying to think and to think straight. Why on earth was Stephen so persistent in saying he had gone to Koblenz? If he *had* gone, he hadn't left Niedernhall until well after eight o'clock.

I reached for a cigarette but my handbag was still indoors. Without thinking I opened Stephen's glove compartment to see if he had left his cigarettes there.

46

The gun was loosely folded in a yellow duster, and visible. It looked brand new. I reached out and touched it lightly with my finger-tips. The cold metal was no figment of my imagination. This, at least, was real.

I was aware of Stephen standing on the opposite side of the road, waiting to cross, and I shut the door on it hastily. Sick and trembling, I stared straight ahead as he opened his door and slipped in next to me. I didn't want to look at him any more. All I wanted to do was go back into the house, shut the door, and try desperately to pretend none of this was happening.

'Here, take these, they'll make you feel better. Perhaps going out this afternoon isn't such a good idea after all. Anyway you'll need this afternoon to pack.'

'Pack!' I faced him in amazement.

'Nothing elaborate. Just enough for two or three days. We can tour around, go where the fancy takes us.'

'I'm sorry. I really can't.'

'Nonsense, Susan. It will be great fun.'

I shook my head. 'No, Stephen, I mean it. I'm not coming.'

I could see two or three cars approaching the village from the direction of Kunzelsau and felt a little better. Gunther wouldn't be much longer and then I could pack my bags and go south, forget completely about Stephen's existence . . .

'Susan, I don't want to make an issue of this, but I want you to come with me.'

It wasn't a request, it was a command.

I forced myself to look straight at him. It was obviously useless to argue. 'All right then,' I agreed. 'Why not?'

Why not indeed? By the time he came for me I would be well on my way to the Alps.

'That's my girl. You won't regret it, I promise you. I'll be back for you about four-thirty. If I were you I'd lie down for a while. Those aspirins should start working soon.'

There was a large red car in the distance, similar to Gunther's heading towards the village . . .

Stephen was saying, 'Well, I'd better be moving. Four-thirty

47

then.'

Mechanically I smiled, went through the motions of saying goodbye to him and stood at the kerb until his car disappeared from view.

The red car turned out to be a Volkswagen loaded with farming materials. I went back to my room and lay once more on the bed, trying to understand the events of the last twenty-four hours. It was stifling hot in the little room and my headache was growing worse.

I supposed that, if their car hadn't crashed, the men would have driven to the farm and hidden out there until the immediate hunt for them was eased. Perhaps Stephen's absence this morning meant that he was removing them from the farm and from the vicinity altogether now that the car had been found. But why was he involved with the assassins of Herr Ahlers? Were his motives political? Financial? . . . And what was this about taking me away for a few days? Stephen knew I could give a description of the men. Was it a trap to get me out of the way, to silence me before I talked? It was possible. Anything was possible. I blinked the sudden tears from my eyes, got off the bed to search for a handkerchief.

The shrill ringing of the telephone interrupted me. I hurried down the wooden stairs, practically snatching the receiver off the hook, convinced it was Gunther. The barely discernible voice of a man said curtly, 'Leave immediately.' Then the line went dead.

I stood rigid, the receiver against my ear, the tide of fear threatening to engulf me completely. Although the voice had been unrecognizable, it hadn't held a German accent.

With trembling hands I dialled Gunther's number. There was no reply. He must still be with the police. I looked at my watch. It was an hour since I'd phoned him. He couldn't be much longer, he just *couldn't*!

I went back to my room, my heart thumping. One thing I could be doing while I waited was to pack my things. I needed no nasty anonymous phone calls to encourage me to leave: the sooner I saw snow and the Alps, the better I'd be pleased. As for Stephen Maitland . . . Charlotte always said I had a lousy taste in men, and for once I agreed with her.

I began flinging skirts and dresses haphazardly into my case and travelling bag, then went in search of Frau Schmidt, to apologize for my abrupt departure. She was nowhere to be found. I put twice the amount of money she would have expected into an envelope and left it in her room with a brief note. I would ask Gunther to explain and apologize for me. Within fifteen minutes I had carried my bags down to the car and had them safely stowed away. I felt the comforting metal of the key-ring in my pocket. A sandwich, a cup of coffee, and I would make my exit. If I went across to the coffee-bar I could see the entrance to the house quite clearly. There would be no danger of my missing Gunther.

For the second time that day I sat at the same window-table. The sandwich, with its generous filling of chicken and chopped ham, would, any other time have been delicious, but I wasn't in the mood to appreciate it at this moment.

A new, unbearable thought was forming slowly in my mind. The more I thought of the events I had so unwittingly been caught up in, the more sinister the 'accident' in the woods seemed. Was it possible that the bullet had really been intended for me? That they knew I had seen them, could identify them? Had I been 'set up', and by Stephen?

The more I thought of it, the more certain I became that the shooting was deliberate. It was all too much of a coincidence, too neat. Stephen's presence on the tail of the killers, his interest in me, the trip out to the isolation of the woods. If the bullet had hit me, it would have been weeks, months even, before I was found. And now his urgency to take me away for a few days . . .

Walking in the direction of Frau Schmidt's, on the far side of the village street, was Christina. I rose from the table, calling to her from the open doorway. Her face broke into a wide grin, and with an acknowledging wave she began to thread her way across the crowded street. I ordered another coffee and went back to wait for her. Her gaiety, when she joined me, was like a breath of fresh air.

'This is most fortunate, Susan. I was just on my way to return your scarf to you.'

'Oh, Christina, I hope you didn't come all this way for that.'

She laughed. 'It was no trouble. My father has gone to Bad Mergentheim and he dropped me off on the way. To tell the truth, I was reluctant to bring it back at all.' She fingered the fine silk enviously. 'It's a beautiful scarf, very Bond Street!'

Impulsively, I said, 'Keep it.'

She looked up, startled. 'I couldn't possibly do that. I didn't mean . . .'

'I know you didn't, but please take it. It will suit you far better than it does me. Red never was my colour.'

She put the scarf over her head, turning to see her reflection in the window.

'Thank you very much, Susan. It's beautiful.'

Then she said innocently, 'I thought you were going out with Stephen today?'

My smile faded. 'There was a change of plan. Actually I'm leaving here today.'

'Oh? Stephen is leaving as well.'

I looked up sharply. 'Are you sure?'

'Yes, I heard him asking my father for his bill this morning.'

I stared at her. It seemed that Mr Maitland and his friends were about to make a speedy withdrawal. Unless they were already in the hands of the police. I glanced at my watch. It was an hour and a half since Gunther had gone to them. It was possible. Any feeling I may have had for the handsome and charming Mr Maitland died a rapid death. Whatever happened to him, he deserved . . .

'I believe Stephen is calling at Oberammergau,' Christina said. 'He made a phone call to the Alte Post this morning.'

'He may only have been phoning a friend there — he seems to have lots of friends scattered about Germany.'

'If it was a friend, he works on the reservation desk.' She

50

stirred her coffee thoughtfully. 'I don't know what's the matter with Stephen this last day or two, he's been like a bear with a sore head.'

It was a little while before either of us spoke again. I was mentally planning a route southwards that would give Oberammergau the widest berth possible, and Christina was pondering on her guest's change of personality. It was a great temptation not to tell her exactly what kind of man the devastating Mr Maitland really was, and why he had such a lot on his mind, but I resisted the urge. She would find out the truth soon enough.

My thoughts were interrupted by her saying cheerily, 'Have a good journey, Susan. I must go now. My father is picking me up at the crossroads at three. There are all the teas to prepare yet, and as for the scarf, I don't know how to thank you. I am glad to have met you.'

I watched her as she walked quickly down the crowded street past Frau Schmidt's, the scarlet headsquare bobbing distinctively between the sombre, black-shawled heads of the village women. It could almost have been myself heading towards the bridge. I glanced once more at my watch. It should be myself. Enough of my holiday had been ruined already. Purposefully I rose and paid the bill. I would go via Kunzelsau, meeting Gunther on the way, or at the police station. I could say goodbye to him there, discharging my public duty at the same time. And make my way to Austria.

The sun was already on its way to the west as I stepped out into the street and walked briskly to my waiting car. The light that had been so piercing was now golden and gentle. It bathed the ancient Town Hall in a warm glow, and danced on the peonies that grew thickly massed in troughs at either side of its front door. In the distance I could see the glint of the slow-moving water beneath the bridge, throwing back reflections of blue and green on to the crumbling stone.

I had reached the car and was already easing it over the cobbled stones when, above the bustle and chatter of everyday street noises, came the sharp squeal of tyres from the far side

51

of the bridge. A terrible scream nearly drowned the simultaneous sound of a car accelerating at great speed.

I froze, skin ice-cold. Then pandemonium broke out as other shouts and cries followed in quick succession and people began running in the direction of the river.

To the left of me, the Burgermeister ran down the steps of the Town Hall, to be joined by a shirt-sleeved man carrying the black bag of a doctor. Together they raced down the street, pushing their way through the crowd who had surged forward, mercifully blocking my view.

After a few long, dreadful minutes, the watching women slowly began to move back across the bridge, standing in small groups in the village street, crossing themselves as they did so. Unwillingly I saw the silent procession approach. The Burgermeister, surrounded by white-faced villagers, was walking back over the bridge, the inert body of a girl in his arms.

It was obvious she was dead. The legs hung at a deformed, improbable angle, the white of the bone showing, her bodice and skirt were saturated in blood. Her head lolled grotesquely, like that of a rag-doll, the scarlet headsquare still knotted beneath her chin. Mechanically I noticed, as the grim cavalcade passed me by, that someone had closed her eyes. Then they were gone; and I was left, sick and terrified, behind the wheel of the car.

'Pardon, Fraulein?' The elderly man from the coffee-bar stooped low, peering concernedly at me. He crossed himself.

'Mother of God. He did not stop.' He repeated it disbelievingly. 'He did not stop.'

'Did you . . . see?' I managed at last.

'Nein. The women say she was walking up the Ohringen Road. This maniac drove into her.' His voice shook. 'But not to stop. It does not seem possible.'

I was vaguely aware of horrified voices outside the car, echoing his words, discussing, speculating. The old man was saying, 'If only she had stayed a little longer in my shop.'

But it would have made no difference. At whatever time

52

Christina had left, wearing my headsquare and looking so much like me, the driver of the car would have followed. Would have killed her . . .

Dimly I heard the old man wish me goodbye and turn to join one of the whispering cliques that now thronged the street. I went through the motions of starting the car. Turned the key in the ignition, pressed my foot on the accelerator. Hardly aware of my actions I motored slowly over the bridge and past the spot where Christina had been murdered in full view of half the population of Niedernhall. Her bag and its contents lay scattered pathetically in the blood-stained dust and dirt of the country road.

Driving crazily I left the village, hills and trees speeding past in an unseen blur. That it should have been my body lying in Niedernhall's Town Hall I hadn't a minute's doubt. And when they found out that it wasn't mine . . .

I gripped the steering wheel hard with clammy hands, forcing myself to be calm. I mustn't panic. A little way ahead I could see the gentle hills and vineyards of Kunzelsau. With a great effort I slowed down, and with Niedernhall lost to view, and Kunzelsau on the horizon, I drew up at the roadside bathed in sweat. I must think. Think.

Chapter Seven

I'm not sure how long I sat there, struggling to get my thoughts in order. I didn't know who had been driving the car that had killed Christina. I didn't know how many people, besides Stephen Maitland and the two men at the farm, were involved. I had seen no one suspicious as she walked away from the safety of the coffee-bar and down the village street, but someone, somewhere, had been watching. One thing I was sure of: I daren't drive openly into Kunzelsau and to the police station. I didn't fancy the odds against my making it. By now, her killer — whoever he was — must have realized his mistake and be looking for me with even more determination than before.

With shaking hands I unfolded my large map of southern Germany and propped it up on the wheel in front of me. To my fevered brain it seemed that all roads led to Oberammergau and under no condition was I going to expose myself and my little Morris on any one of them. Not if Stephen Maitland was making his way to Oberammergau.

I hunted in my shoulder-bag for the leaflet extolling the virtues of the surrounding hamlets and villages as quiet holiday retreats. On the back was a detailed map of the country roads connecting Niedernhall, Kunzelsau, Ohringen and, some miles to the south-east, Schwabisch Hall.

If I took that road, and on reaching Schwabisch Hall phoned Gunther, either at the police station or at his home, then he would come for me and escort me in safety.

Nervously I looked behind me, but the road, flanked by apple trees and summer flowers, was empty, the whole countryside peaceful and still. If I could make it to the right turning for Schwabisch Hall then I was safe. No one would ever think of looking for me there. Hastily I folded the map and started the car. About a hundred yards ahead was the junction, and with a feeling of overwhelming relief I swung the car over, disappearing down it like a rabbit into its hole.

The road was quiet, the only other traffic being farm vehicles and one or two commercial vans. No menacing car loomed up behind me. I stopped at the first telephone box I saw and dialled Gunther's number. The relief when he answered was overwhelming.

'Gunther. Oh, Gunther, thank goodness you're in!'

'Susan! Where are you? You promised to stay at Frau Schmidt's. I've been most worried.'

I said weakly, 'I'm on the outskirts of Schwabisch Hall. I had to leave. Someone . . . killed . . . Christina, the girl from Stephen Maitland's guest-house, in mistake for me.'

I heard his quick intake of breath, then he said, *'Lieber Gott.* So that's it. The whole village is talking of nothing else. But I don't understand. Why should they think she was you?'

'She was wearing my headsquare.'

'I see,' he said slowly. He hesitated for a second then said: 'Susan, listen to me carefully. Drive into Schwabisch Hall and make your way to the Waldlust Bar — it is in the main street, just after the traffic lights. I'll meet you there.'

'Yes,' I said waveringly. 'And, Gunther, please hurry.'

'Don't worry, *meine Liebe,* I'll be there in ten minutes.'

Numbly I put down the receiver and walked back to my car. All the time I was driving through the tree-lined streets I tried to ignore what so far had been left unsaid.

Only Stephen had seen me wear the scarf. Only Stephen . . . I slammed on the brakes to avoid an oncoming car. The driver wound his window down, shouting un-pleasantly as I backed out of the one-way street.

Determinedly I concentrated on my driving and five minutes later parked in a quiet side street some yards from the bar. I picked up my shoulder-bag and map. I could ponder over the quickest and safest route either to Austria or to home, while waiting for Gunther.

A short flight of steps led down into the small and dimly-lit bar. High-backed wooden seats separated each table from its neighbour, but all were unoccupied. I ordered a cognac from a disinterested young man behind the bar who was immersed in a book and obviously resented my interruption, and sat in the corner, shielded by the high back and arm of the chair.

I spread the map out in front of me and tried to concentrate. But superimposed on the roads, railways and towns of Germany, was Stephen Maitland's face. Two dark brown eyes under their black brows stared up at me as I tried vainly to plot a route south. It was impossible. Time and time again I began tracing the bright red lines on the map with a pen, only to find I was sitting with my hand stationary and my thoughts in turmoil. In the end I gave up trying and drank my cognac, bravely interrupting the barman from his book to ask for another.

'Susan!' Gunther ran down the steps, and in front of the slightly more interested barman took me in his arms.

'Thank God you're all right! When Frau Schmidt told me you had gone I didn't know what to think.' He stepped away from me, holding me at arms' length. 'You're trembling, Susan. Here, take your drink and sit down.'

I sat down gratefully, and he joined me, removing one of my hands from the glass I held, taking it in his and holding it tightly.

'If you knew how worried I've been these last few hours, Susan.'

'And if you knew how scared I've been . . . '

'There's no need to be scared any more. The police have arrested them.'

'All . . . of them?'

He nodded grimly. 'Maitland as well. You were quite right. He was in it up to his neck.'

I concentrated very hard on not being sick. 'And Christina?' I asked faintly. 'Do the police know who killed her?'

'The hit and run car was parked at the farm. There's no need to worry about anything now. It's all over.'

I wanted to ask whose car it had been, but the words stuck in my throat.

'I've kept you out of this affair, at least as far as the police are concerned, Susan. You're quite free to continue your holiday.'

I squeezed his hand gratefully. 'Gunther, I don't know what I would have done without you. You've been marvellous.'

'Are you going to stay here a little longer? I would like it if you did.' The blue eyes held mine. I shook my head.

'No, Gunther. I couldn't. Not after what's happened. I'd keep seeing her there.'

'And if I suggested that I come south with you?'

I fingered the glass, trying to think of the right words to say.

'I see,' he said. 'Well, never mind, Susan. One cannot win all the time.' White teeth flashed in a sudden smile. 'But one thing you do owe me is your company for the rest of today. Why not settle for Augsburg? I could drive there with you, book you into a hotel, and then we could have dinner and spend the rest of the evening together. We'll be there by seven. Naturally, I shall depart promptly at the stroke of twelve.'

I laughed. 'All right.'

He rose from the table. 'Then come along, there is no time to lose. It's five o'clock already.'

I picked up my things and followed him into the street.

'It might be a good idea if we telephoned from here and booked you a room,' Gunther said. 'I know just the hotel.'

I was quite happy to let him make all the arrangements, and leaned against the wall in the warmth of the late afternoon sun while he rang Augsburg from the telephone kiosk, trying desperately not to think of Stephen Maitland.

Gunther emerged smiling. 'Dinner for two tonight. Bed and breakfast for one. Where did you park your car?'

'Heavens, I'd nearly forgotten it! It's round the back.'

Gunther's Mercedes straddled the street. I looked at it doubtfully.

'Will I be able to keep up with you?'

57

'Not for a minute. However, with will-power I shall be able to slow down to your speed. You collect your car and follow me.'

Obediently I hurried for my old Morris and joined him a few minutes later. He leaned a blond head out of his window.

'Ready?'

'You bet.'

He laughed and started up the car, and I followed closely behind as we sped through Schwabisch Hall, taking the main road south that led through Nordlingen, Donauworth and to Augsburg. I glanced at the map spread out on the seat beside me, noticing with bitter irony that from Augsburg the road led straight south to Oberammergau.

With an effort I pushed Stephen Maitland to the back of my mind. The whole affair was finished with. I could forget him completely. In time I might even be able to pretend that nothing had happened at all. That is, I could have done if it hadn't been for Christina. Tears pricked my eyelids and I swore out loud. Damn. Damn everything. I forced myself to concentrate on the road ahead, forced myself to think of anything, anything at all, but the nightmare events of the afternoon.

As it happened, following Gunther required all my attention. My car was used to pottering along at thirty-five to forty miles an hour, a speed Gunther would have thought of as stationary. He may have considered he was travelling steadily, but my Morris was flat out with the effort of keeping him in sight.

Within a very short space of time the medieval buildings of Nordlingen, gleaming white against a backdrop of dark fir trees, loomed up ahead of us, Nordlingen's high tower rising splendidly above its walls and bastions, the steps of its street fountains crowded with young people sitting in the sun. I would have liked to slow down and take a closer look at this Imperial Free city which had remained unchanged for centuries, but Gunther was speeding through it, totally oblivious to its charms. I needn't have worried. Fate gave me my wish. The cobbled streets proved too much for the Morris, and with strained noises issuing from beneath the bonnet, she gave an ominous shudder and began to lose speed. I pressed my foot down harder but it was useless. We ground ignominiously to a halt.

Gunther was already lost to view, but a few minutes later the red Mercedes reconnoitred the narrow street, drawing up opposite me. Dejectedly I opened the car door and sat there waiting for him, wondering what else could possibly go wrong.

'She just stopped,' I explained.

Judging by the expression on his face, his thoughts were exactly the same as mine. Exercising admirable self-control he refrained from making any remark and swung the bonnet open, while I tapped my feet listlessly on the cobbles and gazed my fill at the medieval timbered buildings on either side of the street. He slammed the bonnet down impatiently.

'I can see nothing wrong with it, Susan.'

'I'm very sorry, Gunther,' I said miserably. 'I shall have to stay here tonight and get the wretched thing fixed.'

He stood silent for a few minutes, gazing malevolently at the car. Then, taking a deep breath, he said, 'Will it start at all?'

I turned the ignition and gave it a try. The engine coughed and the car crawled forward slowly. He grunted.

'That will have to do. I'll take it to a garage and see what they say before we make any rash decisions. I'm determined our last evening together shall be a memorable one. We don't want to spend it amid these crumbling ruins if we can help it.'

It didn't seem to be the time or place to point out that visitors in their thousands came to enjoy and appreciate the ruins in question, so I silently let him take my place at the wheel.

'Sit in my car till I get back. With a bit of luck it may turn out to be something quite simple.'

As luck had seemingly deserted me since I'd set foot on German soil I didn't share his optimism, but obediently went and sat in the comfort of the Mercedes, suppressing a smile at

59

the sight of the elegant Gunther chugging at a dizzy five miles an hour up the street and round the corner in search of a garage.

It seemed rather a waste of time to be sitting in the car with so many attractions outside and a few minutes later I began to stroll up the street in the direction Gunther had gone.

Gazing idly in the shop windows, being jostled by the crowds, I began to feel like the tourist I really was. I reached the corner Gunther had rounded but there was no sign of him. Succumbing to the magic that the sights and sounds of a strange city always kindles in me, I wandered slowly down the street.

There were many emblazoned signs hanging above the pavement and I stopped to look closer at one above an armourer's. It was richly gilded, supported by a fine wrought-iron pole heavily ornamented with twists and curls and with painted flowers and leaves in each curve. As I stood, back to the road, studying the inn sign, some sixth sense made me stiffen and I turned my head slightly.

Motoring down the street was a white sports car, and behind the wheel was the unmistakable figure of Stephen Maitland.

I froze, unable to think for the panic that swept over me. The car came closer. He would be bound to see me. With mouth dry and heart pounding I turned, head down, hurrying along the crowded pavement. As I reached the corner I could see the car draw parallel with me as it slowed down to negotiate the turn. I stepped into the shadow of a doorway, my back to the road. It wasn't until then that I realized he would have to pass Gunther's Mercedes. It wasn't the most inconspicuous car in the world. He would see it, put two and two together, know I was here. I choked back the hysterical sobs that rose in my throat. What was he *doing* here, for goodness sake? Gunther had said they'd all been arrested. *All* of them, Maitland as well.

I forced myself to peer round the corner. I had been quite right. Stephen Maitland had pulled up directly behind the

Mercedes and was standing like the demon king himself, searching the crowds, looking for me.

Hastily I stepped back. I must find Gunther. There couldn't be so many garages in Nordlingen, and he would have gone to the nearest one. Frantically dredging up all the German I was capable of, I stopped a middle-aged man in working clothes.

'Wo ist die nachste Garage?'

'Links an der Strassenkreuzung.' Seeing the blank look on my face he pointed back the way I had come, using sign language to indicate its whereabouts. I hardly let him finish before I was haring off up the street, dodging between the browsing shoppers.

Further on, past the inn sign I had been looking at, was an obscure turning. I gave an apprehensive glance over my shoulder, then scurried down it. It was a narrow, winding lane, completely deserted, with no pavement of shops, and tall houses rising directly from the cobbles – the perfect place for an unfortunate accident.

I hugged the walls, keeping as far in the shadow as possible, knowing that if Stephen looked down he couldn't help but see me. I broke into a run, my high-heeled sandals ringing out loudly, the sound seeming, to my nervous ears, to echo and re-echo from wall to wall.

Ahead of me I could see an intersection, with a red-roofed inn on the corner, but still no sign of a garage. Had the man said turn to the right or left? I couldn't remember and glanced feverishly behind me, as above the noise of my sandals I heard the soft tread of a man's foot, but it was only a business-man, briefcase tucked respectably under his arm.

It seemed to take me an age to reach the corner and the flower-decked exterior of the inn with its eaves and shutters, but there, not twenty yards away down the left hand turn, was the large sign of a garage. As I neared it, I saw my Morris and the comforting sight of a broad-shouldered Gunther stepping out of a telephone kiosk. At the sound of my running footsteps he looked up, his expression changing to one of alarm.

'Susan, what's the matter?'

For the second time that day his arms were round me, comforting and protective.

Breathlessly I said, 'He's here. Stephen Maitland. I've just seen him.'

It was the first time I had seen Gunther visibly shaken. He looked frankly disbelieving. 'He can't be: it's not possible.'

'But he *is*, and what's more he knows we're here. He's pulled up behind your Mercedes.'

I thought Gunther was going to choke. Instead, he issued a string of expletives that fortunately I couldn't understand, then seized my arms.

'Come on.'

'No! *Please,* Gunther, no! He's dangerous and there are only two of us.' Even to my own ears my voice sounded on the verge of hysteria.

He paused, then patted my arm soothingly. 'He can't harm you here. It's crowded with tourists.'

'It was *market* day at Niedernhall,' I cried, 'and that didn't make any difference!'

He looked down at me, then said gently, 'You're quite right, Susan. You've been through enough already. Though how the hell he came to be here . . . I'll ring the police, they're the people to handle it.'

'They don't seem to be handling it very well so far.'

'Hey, steady on.' He drew me closer, his arm around my shoulders. 'I'm here, remember?'

I smiled sheepishly.

'There's a good girl. I won't be a minute. The police have to be told, they'll be looking for him anyhow. It won't take them long to pick him up.' He gave me a reassuring squeeze and slipped back into the telephone kiosk.

The mechanic, unaware of the drama being enacted around him, whistled tunelessly and continued to tinker with my car. I sat on the wall, recovering some of my lost composure while Gunther spoke angrily on the telephone to the police. His face was still flushed when he replaced the receiver, but his voice when he spoke to me was as gentle and considerate as ever.

'Curtains for Mr Maitland, and an unavoidable change of plan for us. It will be two hours before your car is roadworthy again. Gottfried, the mechanic here, tells me there is a new hotel that has just opened a little way out of town. I took the liberty of cancelling our previous arrangements!'

I nodded passively. Anywhere. I didn't care as long as the spectre of Stephen Maitland was laid at last.

'You can't go back for your car yet, Gunther. Not till . . . not till they've picked him up.'

Gunther was deep in thought and for a moment I thought he was going to disagree with me. Instead he said, 'You're quite right. We'll get a cab over there and I'll come back for my car after dinner.'

He strolled over to Gottfried and asked him to ring for a cab for us. I took a packet of cigarettes from my shoulder-bag and lit one, inhaling deeply. I was beginning to feel better already. A nice, leisurely dinner, a bottle of wine and the knowledge that Stephen Maitland was safely incarcerated behind iron bars was all I needed to ensure a good night's rest. I collected my overnight bag from the rear of the Morris, and within minutes the taxi arrived and we were safely enclosed in its dim and shabby interior.

It seemed to take a lifetime for the taxi-driver to negotiate the narrow, busy street. From the depths of the corner where I had buried myself I searched the crowds, dreading to see the familiar, dark head of hair among the swarms of carefree villagers and tourists. At long last, without any further sight of Stephen Maitland, we shook the dust of the town off our heels and I slowly relaxed.

The sun was beginning to set now, spilling its rosy light on the fields of vines that spread out on either side of us, deepening into a fiery red glow as it silhouetted the still woods of fir and pine that crowned every hilltop. On one, a ruined castle clung tenaciously, the slit windows keeping watch, as they had for centuries, on the winding road below. Only now there were no bands of starving peasants or richly dressed

63

nobles to frown down upon, only the cars of indifferent tourists speeding unheedingly by to more spectacular attractions.

Our destination turned out to be a tiny hamlet in deserted countryside, some two miles from Nordlingen. A handful of pretty, but uninhabitable sixteenth-century cottages surrounded the newly-built hotel that had been deposited in their midst. Its steel and glass frame rose incongruously against the gently sloping hills. Three solitary apple trees, like sentinels, grew on the steeply rising high ground behind it, their spare branches and dark green leaves doing their utmost to soften the building's harsh, metallic lines.

Gunther gave a sigh of satisfaction. 'It looks as if we may have struck lucky after all.'

I kept my thoughts to myself. It didn't matter how monstrous an exterior the hotel presented; inside would be safety and a chance to recover my badly shaken equilibrium. Tomorrow morning would see me setting off well rested and composed, instead of in the state of nervous collapse I seemed so frequently to be nearing.

Austria, with its beautiful scenery and remnants of a great empire, lay temptingly before me. Gunther squeezed my shoulder gently, and from my reverie of the splendid and magnificent palaces of the Hapsburgs, I was faced with the stark reality of the hotel's ultra-modern and garish entrance hall.

Chapter Eight

Gottfried hadn't been exaggerating when he had said the hotel was brand new. Amid the angular furniture and expensive draperies were signs of a very recent retreat by the builders. The smell of sawdust still hung in the air and ladders and tins of paint were stacked in one corner.

But when I had been shown to my room, and felt the luxury of the sprung mattress after the archaic one at Frau Schmidt's, and when I had seen the mauve and lilac bathroom and the unending hot water that gushed from the freshly plastered taps, I forgave all. To slip my tired body into the depths of the fragrant water was sheer bliss. I lay back, eyes closed, taut muscles gradually relaxing.

After a long soak I wound one of the large, thick bath towels provided by the proprietors round my damp body and padded back into the bedroom. With infinite care I made up my face, disguising the signs of strain that still remained, brushing my hair into a high, sophisticated chignon, concentrating on each single action and refusing point blank to dwell on Christina's hideous death. There would be plenty of time for that. Too much time. But later . . . later I would be able to cope better. If I surrendered to the memory now I would be finished. So I sprayed perfume behind my ears and on my throat, took a deep, steadying breath, and went in search of Gunther.

He was in the cocktail bar, staring out of the large picture-window at the shadowy depths of the valley and the opposite hills, now barely discernible in the dusk. He turned at my approach.

'*Very* nice,' he said, eyeing me appraisingly. 'I like your hair like that. It is very becoming.' His arm slid round my shoulders. 'Dinner is ready whenever you are. We can have an apéritif at the table.'

'Good. I'm ready for dinner now. I've not eaten properly all day.'

He laughed. 'Come along then. You're too beautiful to go hungry.'

Taking my arm he led the way through an arched doorway into the dining-room. It, too, showed signs of recent completion.

'I'm not the first guest they've had, am I?' I asked dubiously, looking at the otherwise empty room.

'Not quite, though when it comes to signing the register I think you will find yourself on the first page.' He passed me the menu. 'The hotel opened officially a week ago. They had a few guests then. Whether they are still here, I don't know. I've seen no one but staff while waiting for you.'

I handed the menu back to him. 'You choose, Gunther. I trust you entirely.'

His hand gripped mine. 'Enough to ask me to stay tonight?'

To my annoyance I felt myself colouring. 'Not . . . the way you mean.'

He said softly, 'You may change your mind before the evening is over.'

To my great relief the waiter came and the subject was dropped, at least temporarily, as Gunther ordered the meal and the wine.

The food was delicious. A delicate, clear soup, followed by trout and then small pieces of tender chicken in a spicy sauce with asparagus tips and button mushrooms, then a concoction of meringue and fresh strawberries followed by a cheeseboard that satisfied even Gunther. He finished the last of the Camembert and wiped his mouth with his napkin.

'This is the part I do not like,' he said.

I looked up, surprised.

'This leaving you and going for the car,' he explained, rising to his feet, a slight frown on his face. 'It's a damn nuisance. Still, it shouldn't take me more than half an hour.' His blond hair gleamed under the soft lights and he looked every girl's idea of a Prince Charming. 'Where will you wait — in the cocktail bar or the lounge?'

'The lounge, I think, with a coffee.'

While I settled myself before the fire in the otherwise deserted lounge, he telephoned for a cab, and when the waiter had brought me a tray with a silver pot of coffee on it, he reluctantly left me.

It was very comfortable sitting, coffee in hand, gazing into the fiery depths of the log fire, but it gave me too much opportunity for thought. I rose restlessly, pacing the room, coming to a halt before the window. The tail lights of Gunther's cab had already disappeared down the narrow, winding road to Nordlingen, there was nothing to be seen, only the inky blackness of the fields and woods.

I was just about to turn and pour myself another cup of coffee, when far down the hillside a light bobbed unevenly, then disappeared. I strained my eyes into the darkness, not sure if I was imagining things. A few minutes later it appeared again, this time nearer. Apprehensively I stiffened, watching intently. The speed and movement indicated that it wasn't a vehicle, in fact it was too far to the left to be on the road at all. Someone was climbing by the light of a torch, up the hillside towards the hotel.

I stepped back quickly, the now familiar feeling of panic mounting. I would go to the manager, ask him to call the police. I hurried across the room, then hesitated, hand on the door-knob. What if it *wasn't* Stephen Maitland? I didn't relish the thought of the fuss and the explanations, and surely . . . surely it couldn't be him?

I re-crossed the room, carefully avoiding the windows, edging along the wall until I was hidden by the heavy folds of velvet curtaining. Steeling myself, I lifted the near edge of the material away from the wall and peeped through the chink. The torchlight had vanished. Several seconds passed, then, just as I was beginning to hope it had all been a figment of my imagination, the light topped the brow of the hill, making straight for the hotel. I held my breath as the blurred outline came nearer and nearer. Even at that distance there was no mistaking him.

I let the curtain fall and ran out into the hallway and to the reception desk. The young man behind it stared uncomprehendingly from behind rimless glasses as I said breathlessly, 'The police, quickly. *Schnell.*'

From behind me came the calm authoritative voice of the manager. He raised a hand to silence the receptionist and smiled benignly at me.

'*Was haben Sie gesagt?*'

'The police, *rufen Sie die Polizei, bitte.*'

Again he smiled, patting my arm soothingly.

With an effort I controlled the shaking in my voice and said, '*Rufen Sie die Polizei, bitte. Bitte.*'

Between the manager and the receptionist passed a look of resigned understanding, but instead of doing as I'd asked, the receptionist rang the desk bell and two maids hurried down the stairs to where we were standing.

The manager spoke to them in German, still patting my arm irritatingly.

Before I knew what was happening I was being politely but firmly, very firmly, escorted towards my room. The generously-built young lady who had taken a firm grip of my left arm was making suitably sympathetic noises and all in all I was being treated as if I was in a mental home, not a hotel.

The more insistent I became, the more force was exercised. The receptionist hurried up with a large brandy and a shaky smile. Angrily I pushed the glass away, the golden drops scattering over the brand new carpet.

By this time we were on the second floor outside the open door of my room. As the five of us jostled in an undignified manner on the landing I saw a bunch of keys in the manager's hand and realized with horror he intended locking the door of my room once I'd gone in.

Too many unbelievable things had happened in the past few days and I was beyond the point of wondering why the staff should be acting in such a preposterous manner. Nothing seemed too bizarre. But one thing I was sure of: I was *not* going to be locked in a hotel bedroom by the manager and his entourage.

I stopped protesting and smiled sweetly. Four astonished faces smiled nervously back. I accepted the drink with thanks, apologized for any inconvenience, and sat passively on the bed. When it seemed apparent that my brainstorm had passed, the two maids were dismissed. Again I smiled, apologized. The manager made understanding noises and he and the receptionist finally made to leave. I went with them to the door, and as the manager attempted to close it, restrained him gently, wiping my forehead and indicating that I would like it open for the air. He eyed me doubtfully. Feeling as if my face would split with the effort, I smiled yet again. With a shrug of the shoulders he assented, and I went back and sat on the bed, sipping the drink as if I hadn't a care in the world, until the two men were out of hearing.

As soon as the last of their footsteps had died away, I leaped up, grabbed my coat, stuffed the few things I had unpacked back into my overnight bag, and peered out of the window. There was no light to be seen now and no welcoming car lights that would have heralded Gunther.

I listened intently for any sounds from the direction of the reception desk but all was quiet. It appeared that Stephen Maitland was, as yet, still outside. But for how long?

He couldn't have walked all the way from Nordlingen: he must have driven to the bottom of the hill and parked his car away from the roadside so that it wouldn't be seen by anyone passing up and down the road.

I remembered the occasion at the farm when he had left the keys in the car. Would he have been so careless again? It was worth taking a risk. I couldn't stay where I was like a rabbit in a trap. Any action was better than none. If I took his car I could meet Gunther and Stephen Maitland would be stranded.

I stepped out on to the landing. There was no one about and the only sounds were muffled ones from the ground floor.

That I wouldn't be able to walk unmolested out of the hotel via the reception desk seemed obvious. So I tiptoed in the opposite direction to the main staircase, following the corridor as it turned left. Two or three doors led off it and at the far end a blank wall rose uncompromisingly. I tried two of the doors on the left hand side, but both were bedrooms with no other means of exit. The third led into a small store-room, and, in the far corner, nearly obliterated by workmen's tools and ladders, was a glass door opening on to a narrow back staircase.

I clambered over the cardboard boxes and packages and hurried down the staircase as fast as I dared, past the first and the ground floor until I was in the basement. In the moonlight that shone weakly through a window on the far side, I could see bags of cement and tins of paint, and, next to the window, a door. Grasping the knob in both hands, and hoping that security at the hotel left a lot to be desired, I turned and pushed.

Within four minutes of leaving my bedroom I was outside on the open hillside.

The evening breeze blew refreshingly on my face. I slipped my arms into my coat sleeves, shut the door quietly behind me and took a firm hold of my overnight bag. The hill on which I was standing swept round in a wide arc, shelving away steeply beneath my feet. The path was only a few feet wide, and I picked my way carefully over the litter and débris that lay on it. Keeping well in, I edged stealthily towards the corner of the building.

I pressed myself back against the wall as I reached it, listening intently for the sound of other footsteps in the darkness, but the only sound was the rustling of the wind as it blew through the apple trees and the long grass.

Heart thumping, I peered round the corner. The narrow path continued down the eastern side of the hotel, blocked only by several shiny dustbins. None of the windows that opened out on to it was lit. Walking softly I skirted the bins and approached the front of the hotel. Here, light from the windows streamed out over the forecourt and the road leading up to it, illuminating the surrounding countryside in pale light for thirty or forty yards.

I hugged the wall, straining my eyes as I peered in the direction the torch had been heading. Nothing moved now. It was completely still.

From inside the hotel came the distant hum of voices, then, as I waited in an agony of indecision, a bedroom light was switched on and stayed on. It appeared that Mr Maitland had booked in.

It was only a matter of minutes across the forecourt to the road, but it was bathed in light and anyone looking out of the hotel windows would be able to see. The safest way would be to stay in the darkness. I didn't relish the idea of clambering down into the black void that surrounded me, but the alternative was too risky. If Stephen Maitland saw me leave, he would be able to catch up with me in minutes.

I stepped off the path and on to the open hillside, plunging steeply downhill. It was dark and the ground was rough. I stumbled and slipped, clutching desperately at stray bushes, the night pressing in on me like a physical force. My foot caught in the twisted roots of a tree and I fell forward with a cry, arms outstretched, clasping the pitted bark. I leaned heavily against it, gasping, rubbing my ankle and listening for the sound of Gunther's returning Mercedes, but all I heard was my own laboured breathing.

The road, now in complete darkness, was a little way to my right and I slithered painfully over to it, sliding amid a flurry of loose stones down the shallow bank and on to the firm gravel.

It was becoming increasingly colder and I hugged my coat round me, running . . . Imaginary shapes and shadows rose up around me, my ankle was hurting, my whole being craved for the sound of Gunther's car. The road dipped suddenly and I slowed down, looking apprehensively towards the hotel. All the lights on the ground floor were still on, only the bedroom light had disappeared.

71

The moon sailed from behind a bank of cloud and, silhouetted in its silver light, was the dark figure of a man, running and leaping down the hillside behind me.

With a sob I whirled round, running harder than ever, frantically searching for his parked car. The road curved once more, levelling and widening into the straight stretch that led into Nordlingen.

I paused, panting and straining my eyes into the blackness. Blindly I headed off the road to the right, half fainting with fatigue and shock, slipping and sliding over the damp grass. Perhaps he would go straight past me, following the road. Perhaps here, in the dark, I would be safe. Heedlessly I scrambled further into the undergrowth, then, in front of me rose the welcoming outline of the Sprite.

I had been right. If only I was right also about the keys! Please, *please* let me be right about the keys, I prayed, as half hysterically I grasped the door handle and turned, nearly falling into the driver's seat. By the time I'd felt the keys in the ignition and turned them, I was sobbing uncontrollably.

The car lurched and swayed over the uneven ground back to the road; as it rocked down the bank of earth I could see the running figure of Stephen Maitland now not more than fifty yards away. I swung the car hard left, pressed my foot down as far as it would go and sent the car bucketing over the ruts and down the wrong side of the road towards Nordlingen and Gunther.

The car felt strange beneath my hands and by the time I'd swerved back to the right side of the road and got it under control all signs of the hotel and the car's rightful owner were far behind me. I wiped the sweat from my forehead and settled down to a steady sixty to sixty-five, keeping a sharp look-out for any oncoming headlights.

The moon hung like an orb in the still sky above me, splashing the fields and occasional cottages with pale golden light as I speeded past them towards the distant outline of the town. Gradually pinpricks of light appeared and then there was the faint glow of street lights. Within minutes I was inside the city walls but still no sign of Gunther. Puzzled, I drove through the cobbled streets to the main thoroughfare where he had left his car. The street was deserted, the car gone.

I halted, staring at the vacant place, a new fear slowly creeping over me. The German police had not succeeded in arresting Stephen. Had he been lying in wait for Gunther's return? Had he come to the hotel *after* seeing Gunther? The gnawing fear became a certainty. I closed my eyes. If Stephen Maitland had been able to force Gunther to tell him my whereabouts, what chance did I have? And where was Gunther now?

Hardly aware of what I was doing I fumbled with the gears and reversed back up the street, taking the left hand turn towards the garage. As I motored down the quiet lane that led to it, it was as if I had been plucked from the sane world of the Twentieth Century and transported back in time to the murderous world of the Middle Ages. Faint strains of music came from the old coaching inn as I turned the corner, and in front of me lights still burned in the garage.

I parked the car and ran across the forecourt to the small office, knocking loudly on the door. It was opened by Gottfried, still covered in oil and grease. He stared at me indifferently.

'Is my car ready, please?'

His expression didn't alter. I tried again. 'My car, is it ready?'

He nodded, wiping his hands on a filthy handkerchief and led the way into the workshop where my Morris stood, bonnet down, ready for the road.

'Could I have my bill, please?'

From the top pocket of his overalls he silently produced a grubby piece of paper. I paid him, my hands trembling as I counted out the notes.

'Has Herr Cliburn been here tonight?'

He looked blankly at me.

'Herr Cliburn, the man who was with me.'

A faint glimmer of understanding crossed his face, then he

shook his head negatively, and began to count the money I had given him. Despairingly I collected my car, parking it a few yards beyond the Sprite.

Gottfried disappeared into the warmth of his office and so, unseen by anyone, I left the Sprite parked at the roadside and, safely installed in my own little Morris, motored off without a backward glance.

It would take Stephen Maitland quite some time to reach Nordlingen without transport, and even longer for him to find his car. By the time he did I would be many, many miles away.

The very familiarity of my own car made me feel safer and I sped purposefully through the deserted streets, past the city gates and on to the main road in the direction of Augsburg.

Chapter Nine

I drove steadily for an hour, and then it started to rain heavily. Before very long the road was awash with water, the car spraying waves of mud in its wake as I forged on.

I peered through the blurred and streaming glass. It was nearly ten-thirty, and I was beginning to feel the effects of the last twenty-four hours. My original idea of driving through the night to Austria was fading rapidly. I kept on for another half hour, the rain falling hollowly on to the roof of the car, the only other sound the continuous rhythmic swish of the wipers as they flicked back and forth. Anti-climax was setting in and I was cold and very, very tired.

I drove through the rain-lashed streets of Augsburg as the city bells tolled eleven, pulling up outside a small hotel. Wearily I trudged into the brightly-lit entrance hall. The receptionist was pleasant, spoke good English and was able to accommodate me for bed and breakfast without any difficulty. I went back to the car, parked it in the hotel's private car park, well away from sight of anyone passing on the road, picked up my overnight bag and followed the receptionist up several flights of stairs to my room.

I must have looked as weary as I felt for she said sympathetically, 'Have you travelled far?'

I was about to say 'no' when I remembered the late hour and nodded. She smiled. 'It is very tiring driving all day, no?'

I agreed wholeheartedly as we began to climb another flight of stairs.

'Your destination, is it Austria?'

I was about to reply non-committally, then said instead: 'I'm going to Switzerland.'

If he traced me as far as here, though without psychic

75

powers I didn't see how it was possible, then the determinedly chatty receptionist could put him on the wrong trail. She opened the door of my room.

'You are very lucky; it is very beautiful there. Beautiful and peaceful.'

I smiled wryly, and after she had wished me good night, I shut the door, locking it securely. Then I began to get ready for bed.

The face that looked back at me from the dressing-table mirror as I removed my make-up was pale and drawn. I put the top back on the jar of cream slowly, studying my reflection. How many days had it been since I had set off carefree and happy for my picnic? Two, three? It seemed another lifetime.

I turned to the bed, noticing for the first time the telephone on the bedside table. I stared at it for a long time, then dialled the number of the hotel at Nordlingen.

'Herr Cliburn, *bitte*.'

Full of foreboding I waited, each second seeming like an hour. That he wouldn't be there to answer I was certain. All I was ringing for was confirmation of the fact. A disembodied voice said something in German then, miraculously, Gunther's voice, harsh and clipped.

For a few seconds I sat foolishly, unable to speak for the constriction in my throat, overwhelmed by relief.

'Gunther! You're all right. You're safe. Oh, I'm so *thankful*.'

Tears splashed down my cheeks. I think it was not till then that I admitted to myself how frightened for him I'd been.

'Susan! Thank God you're safe. Where on earth are you?'

'Augsburg.'

'*Augsburg*!' he shouted. 'Would you mind explaining to me what you are doing there and why you left the hotel in such an extraordinary manner?'

'But I *had* to. Stephen Maitland came to the hotel. I asked the manager to call the police but he behaved in a most peculiar manner.'

'According to the manager it was you who behaved in a

peculiar manner. There's been no sign of Maitland here tonight.'

'But I *saw* him.'

Gunther took a deep breath and said patiently, 'And after you saw him?'

'Well, you weren't back and the staff weren't helpful, so I left by the back staircase. Gunther, he followed me down that hillside. If it wasn't for the fact that his car was parked at the bottom of the hill and I took it . . . '

'You took his car?'

'I had to. Then I drove to Nordlingen expecting to meet you on the way. When I didn't, and saw that your car was gone I thought . . . ' I faltered. 'I thought he'd waylaid you.'

'*Him*! Waylay me!' Gunther's voice was scornful.

'Well, what else was I to think? I collected my car from the garage, left his in the street, and drove here.'

'I see,' said Gunther slowly, and I sensed him coming to a decision. 'And where, exactly, is here?'

I looked at the headed notepaper beside the telephone.

'The Hotel St Wolfgang.'

'Susan, listen to me carefully. On *no* account, I repeat on no account are you to leave there until I've seen you. Understand?'

'Yes, but . . . '

'No buts. You stay at the hotel till I come. I'll be there before you have breakfast.'

'Yes, Gunther, but . . . '

'*You . . . stay . . . there*!' he shouted down the phone.

'Yes,' I said meekly. 'And, Gunther, I'm so glad, so very glad you're all right.'

His voice softened. 'The agonies I have suffered since I found you gone are indescribable, Susan. I don't want to spend another three hours like the last three ever again. I'll see you in the morning.'

'Yes. Good night, Gunther.'

'Good night, *Liebling*.'

Gently I put down the phone and climbed into bed, still

hardly able to believe he was safe. I turned off the bedside light, snuggling further down under the blankets. It appeared that Stephen Maitland had never entered the hotel, so that while I had been clambering in the darkness down the hillside, he must have been very near to me. I shivered, the hideous feeling of being hunted still all too real. How had he known where we were? My tired brain struggled to think clearly, then gave up the effort, and I drifted off into a restless sleep.

The bars of sunlight spilling through the shuttered windows woke me early. For a few minutes I lay, cocooned in the luxurious comfort of the soft bed, gazing around the strange room.

Nordlingen? Augsburg? Slowly my befuddled brain began to function and the events of the previous evening flooded back with painful clarity. I groaned and rolled over, burying my head in the pillows. Today I would free myself for good from Stephen Maitland's pursuit. I felt better as I remembered Gunther's promise to be here by breakfast time and groped at the side of my bed for my watch. It was only six o'clock, but all vestiges of sleep had vanished.

I padded over to the shutters, flinging them wide, letting the early morning sunlight fill the room. White clouds hung wispily above, and the air felt fresh and sweet after the previous night's rain. I washed and dressed slowly, enjoying to the full the feeling of safety and security the little-known hotel gave me. There wasn't the remotest possibility of Stephen Maitland, or anyone else, following me here. For once I could relax and stop looking behind me.

I rang for room service, asked for morning coffee and lay back on the bed, propped up comfortably against the many pillows. Then, listening to the early morning street sounds and the pleasant singing of the birds that drifted through the open window, I lit a cigarette, watching the blue smoke spiral to the ceiling, wondering which road south to take when I left after breakfast and whether the purpose of Herr Cliburn's visit was to ask if he could accompany me.

The maid came in with the coffee and a cheery *'Guten*

Morgen.' I took the tray from her, putting it on the bedside table, and spread out my map of southern Germany on the bed. The first problem, at least, I could solve here and now. The second would have to wait until after breakfast.

The main road south from Augsburg led straight to Oberammergau. That was the road anyone following me would expect me to take, and was the destination the receptionist believed me to be heading for. Intently I searched for more desirable ways of entering Austria. The only real alternative was to head south-east via Munich. I frowned. Normally I always avoided large cities, but normality had vanished days ago. Munich it would have to be.

From downstairs I could hear doors opening and closing, and I went in search of food. Early though it was, I still wasn't the first down to breakfast. A couple of businessmen sat at separate tables and at the large table near the window was a young family, unmistakably French. There were three sun-tanned children dressed in tee-shirts and shorts, and a curly-headed toddler dressed in hardly anything at all, enjoying a noisy, and for the Continent, hearty breakfast.

I contented myself with freshly baked rolls served with tiny pots of jam and more of the deliciously hot coffee. The middle-aged man at the next table flicked open a morning paper and I peered across, trying to see if the headlines were still about the shooting of Herr Ahlers, but he was reading the business columns. He turned as I looked over his shoulder, freezing me with an austere stare, pointedly moving the paper to the far side of his table.

Suitably chastened, I concentrated on buttering another roll and decided that, after my breakfast, I would stroll down to the nearest newsagent's and buy a selection of the morning's press. A place like Augsburg would probably have English newspapers.

The children scampered to the door, watched disapprovingly by the man on my left. Through the window I could see them being bundled into a shabby Bentley piled high with luggage.

Laughing and chattering they disappeared out of the car park and down the main street. I smiled to myself as I picked up my shoulder-bag; they, at any rate, had no troubles. With a little luck, my troubles too would soon be over.

I left a message at the reception desk for Gunther in case he arrived before I got back, and followed the sour-faced German businessman down the front steps.

The streets of Augsburg were already alive with early-morning shoppers, and a pavement artist sat working in the shade of a large, sun-dappled oak tree. The enticing smell of newly baked bread filled the air as I passed him with a smile and strolled along in search of a newsagent's. I crossed a cobbled square and beneath the palisade of trees at the far side was a flower stall ablaze with colour, and next to it a street stand creaking with newspapers and glossy magazines.

Hopefully I scanned the titles for an English one but without success. I selected half a dozen dailies at random and began leafing through them as I set off at a slightly brisker pace back to the hotel. If Gunther found me missing when he arrived this morning, he would have every right to be annoyed.

The very first page I looked at had a photograph of the car the two men had abandoned, and though I couldn't understand much of the accompanying newsprint, it appeared that all the papers had the same story to tell. They all contained photographs of the car before it was wrecked, and the inside pages were given over to scenes from the shooting.

I was so intent on trying to decipher the captions beneath the photographs that I did not hear the soft purr of the car approaching. Or, if I did, I paid no attention to it, but kept on walking, head buried in the newspaper.

Without warning a shadow fell across me. Too late then to suspect that danger lurked even in the quiet streets of Augsburg. I opened my mouth to scream, as my arms were wrenched behind me, the sheaf of papers scattering to the ground. Before I could utter a sound, a sickly sweet pad was pressed over my nose and mouth, and like a small child, I fell without a struggle or sound to the enemy.

Chapter Ten

I was submerged; drowning beneath a great weight; filled with a nameless and unspeakable horror as grotesque shapes marched menacingly through my unconscious mind. Dimly I was aware of movement, the sickening, repetitive sensation of rising and falling and all the time armies without form or face pressed in, suffocating and strangling me.

From a far, immeasurable distance came the sound of distorted voices and the legion of evil that assailed me from all sides slowly receded. I became vaguely aware of light filtering into the dark recesses of my numbed brain and the smell and feel of leather against my face. Hazily I focused on the dark red of the cracked seat on which I lay, struggling vainly to rid myself of the last threads of my nightmare and regain full consciousness. The sickly sweet smell that had pervaded the darkness I had just escaped from hung round me like thick fog. I turned my head, searching for fresh air and tried to raise a hand to wipe my parched lips. Only once more I was aware of a restraining force. As I struggled uselessly to move my immobile arm the last vestiges of unconsciousness were swept away and my mind slowly registered the fact that my hands and feet were firmly bound.

I shook my head, trying to bring into focus the blurred outline of rotting orange peel and half-smoked cigarettes that scattered the floor a mere eighteen inches away. Superimposed on the unrecognizable voices was the familiar sound of changing gears and the rhythmic drone of a car engine. With difficulty I moved my head back, my eyes sliding up over the grey wall in front of me, until they rested on strange heads and shoulders.

Reality engulfed me like a cold sea. I must have cried aloud as I understood at last where I was and what had happened. The man in the passenger seat turned, looking down at me with a smile as I lay like a trussed chicken, completely helpless, amid the decaying litter, being carried God only knew where.

He leaned towards me, one arm resting on the back of his seat. He looked even more unpleasant close to than when I had last seen him through my binoculars after he had crashed the car. He was heavy-jowled with thick, fleshy features and small eyes that were all but submerged in the surrounding folds of fat as the big, slack mouth widened in an even broader smile.

'Our passenger is not happy, Harvey,' he said sarcastically, his eyes travelling the length of my bound body. His companion merely grunted.

The thought of how I had been manhandled filled me with a blind, consuming anger that left no room for fear. I heard myself saying, 'How *dare* you! How *dare* you treat me like this. Untie me this minute.'

The man watching me threw back his head, his large body convulsed with laughter as he wiped genuine tears of mirth from his eyes. At last he recovered himself sufficiently to say jeeringly, 'And what will you do? What dreadful fate will befall us if we do not do as you ask? You are going to teach us both a lesson, eh?'

The very idea caused a fresh explosion of laughter in which the driver joined. I struggled in vain to sit up.

'You'll be laughing on the other side of your face before I've finished,' I said furiously, twisting first one way then another in an effort to reach a sitting position. The laughter .ceased as suddenly as it had begun. He thrust his head forward, eyes like beads, the pitted flesh of his cheeks hanging loosely like an ageing bulldog's.

'You had better learn some manners, young lady. You had better be careful.'

At the menace in his voice, I shrank back and tried desperately not to show the fear that at last filled me. For what seemed like several minutes he glared at me, his face only inches away, cold eyes probing mine. I stared back as contemptuously as I could.

He shook his head slowly. 'Be *very* careful. You have caused far too much trouble already. People are getting tired of you. *Very* tired. You would find it greatly to your advantage if you co-operated. For instance, that cord. If you were to be a sensible girl . . . '

'Don't be a bloody fool,' the man called Harvey said sharply.

Ignoring the interruption the other continued, 'If you were to promise to be a sensible girl, we might untie you.' He eyed my chaffed wrists and ankles which were already beginning to swell painfully. 'You don't look very comfortable, or — ' he slobbered — 'ladylike.'

'Go to hell!' I said, in the most unladylike manner possible.

His smile vanished abruptly and for an instant I thought he was going to strike me.

'For Christ's sake don't let her antagonize you. Things are bad enough already,' the driver said angrily. 'Ignore the stupid bitch.'

With an agreeing grunt my tormentor turned his back on me and we continued in silence. I lay inert on the back seat of the car, trying to get my panic-stricken thoughts in some sort of order. From where I lay I could see very little of the passing countryside but what I could see suggested we were travelling north, not south.

Back to Niedernhall? And if so, why? And who had the German police arrested for the killing if both these men *and* Stephen Maitland were still at large?

It didn't make any sense at all. I stared at the backs of the men's necks, wondering with rising hysteria if one of them had been driving the car that had killed Christina. That I was to have the same fate seemed obvious. Somehow, despite all that had happened, they were free. It could only mean that the police didn't know their identities after all, else they would never be taking the risk of driving openly on the highway. I was still the only one who knew. I would have to be silenced.

83

My only chance was Gunther. When he arrived at the hotel and found me missing he would suspect what had happened. I shivered. That was if Gunther hadn't been taken care of too.

If I was to get away, then I would have to do it before we reached our destination, and I stood no chance while bound hand and foot. With a struggle I swallowed my pride and said, 'Are you going to untie me then or not?'

He turned. 'Are you going to be sensible?'

I nodded. Again the man driving made a sound of protest but it was swept aside and the big man leaned over the back of his seat, taking a penknife from his pocket. His heavy body hung sweatily over mine as he see-sawed at the thick twine. Finally it snapped, and breathing heavily, he slid back into his seat. I rubbed my swollen wrists in an effort to get the circulation moving again.

He watched me, a wet smile on his lips, as I gingerly began massaging my ankles.

'You will find it always easier if you co-operate.'

The man at the wheel gave a short laugh. 'You're a fool, Ivan. Being nice to her will get you no favours.'

Ivan swung round in his seat with a scowl.

Tentatively I sat up. Ivan spoke with an accent but the man at the wheel was English and was the same florid-faced, tweeded and brogued figure I had followed through the streets of Niedernhall. Despairingly I stared out of the window. My earlier surmise was confirmed. The countryside we were passing through wasn't that of the south. We were travelling north.

Ahead of us were a few scattered cottages, the sun shining on white plastered walls, and a few minutes later we were driving through the outskirts of a small market town. Hope surged through me. A town meant people. If I could only draw attention to my plight, if there were any police about . . .

As if reading my thoughts, Ivan turned. 'I wouldn't bother if I were you. If you cause us any trouble we shall have no alternative but to shut you up.' He leered. 'Permanently.'

He said it as casually as if he were making an observation

about the weather. I closed my eyes, not wanting him to see the defeat that must be showing in them.

None of this could possibly be happening to me. It was a bad dream, a nightmare from which I must soon, surely, wake . . .

The car slowed down as it reached the busy streets of the town centre. I opened my eyes as it stopped altogether. Before us was a queue of traffic and a policeman on point duty. Slowly we inched forward and I surreptitiously edged my hand towards the door handle. This might be the one and only chance I would get. Around us cars and cyclists hooted impatiently and I steeled myself to make the break, to fling the door open at the exact moment we passed the policeman. The sun gleamed on his helmet and we were now so near that I could see the beads of sweat on his face. I gripped the handle with clammy hands . . .

'You do, girl, and you're dead.'

Ivan had half-turned, his right hand rested on the edge of his seat, and in it, pointing directly at me, was a small black pistol.

I froze. He could be bluffing but it was a risk I wasn't taking. The policeman raised his arm waving us on and we edged past him, swinging to the right down the main thoroughfare, picking up speed as we did so. My chance had gone. The signpost at the next crossroads indicated Stuttgart to the north, Augsburg to the east, Reutlingen to the west. We went straight on, towards Stuttgart.

I tried to recreate a map of southern Germany in my mind. Stuttgart could not be more than thirty-five to forty miles away from Niedernhall. If the village was to be our destination we would be there in under an hour.

Outside the sun shone hotly down on the hills and fields that fled past with sickening speed. The small towns of Geislingen and Goppingen came and went. Then we were enmeshed in the mean suburban streets of Stuttgart and still there had been no opportunity to escape. Suddenly the man at the wheel, the man named Harvey, spoke.

85

'I imagine you will have plenty to say to Mr Maitland when you see him again.'

'That,' I said, flushing with anger, 'is the understatement of the year.'

He frowned. 'You have caused us all a lot of inconvenience, Miss Carter. I would be careful of your attitude.'

I didn't deign to reply, and he gave a shrug, returning his attention to the road.

I stared at his reflection in the mirror stonily. The red-veined cheeks and thick, well-tended handle-bar moustache didn't look as if they belonged to a man who was a killer. I wondered what his reaction would be if I told him I had no intention of going to the police, that if only he would let me go, I would forget all about them, never mention the affair to a living soul. He glanced up and his eyes held mine for a second. Looking into their cold, green depths, even that hope faded. I would get no help from that quarter.

The road began to run parallel with a river, straddled at intervals by soft pink bridges. The trees lining its banks were reflected in the still, deep waters as it flowed gracefully down to the Rhine. Another town, small and insignificant, came and went, leaving an impression of small courtyards decked with ivy and a statue of Kaiser Wilhelm II in the market square. The signposts on the outskirts indicated Heilbronn.

Sweat broke out on my forehead. We were nearly there.

I breathed deeply. Scared to death I may be, but I was damned if I was going to let these men see it. The landscape became uncomfortably familiar. Before long I could see the pointed steeple of Niedernhall's small church, the sun gilding the roofs of the houses that clustered beneath its protection. But that protection did not extend to me and we turned abruptly to the left, heading down the narrow lane that led towards the farm. At the end of the lane the car turned right on to the roughly beaten track that climbed between the trees until we emerged on the bare hillside below the farm. Here the track levelled out, leading through iron gates to the front of the house.

My heart beat painfully as we halted in the corner of the paved yard. Ivan turned. 'Come on. Out. And don't make a run for it. You won't get very far.'

I opened the door and stood shivering in the warm sunlight. The whole house had an aura of desolation and emptiness, with dark-green tentacles of ivy stretching across the small-paned windows.

It was completely isolated. There was no other house in sight, only the thickly-wooded lower slopes stretching down into the valley, hiding the road and the nearby village from view. Our footsteps rang out hollowly on the stone flags as I allowed myself to be led towards the large, oak door. Here was where my journey came to an end. Perhaps literally, I thought with horror.

Chapter Eleven

I stood hemmed in between them as Harvey knocked loudly on the door. From the rooftop came the sound of pigeons coo-ing and the flutter of their wings as they flew out from under the eaves to the outbuildings that edged the far side of the yard. Vaguely I was aware of the birds singing in the distance, of the warm sun on my back and the light breeze pulling at my hair, but it seemed to be someone else who stood in front of the closed door, held firmly with unfriendly hands.

With a curse Harvey fumbled in his pocket for a key. I was dimly aware of him saying, 'Where the bloody hell is he?' as I was led, nearly insensible, across the threshold and into a flagged hallway.

The sound of the heavy door slamming shut behind us jolted me out of my numbed reverie. Of all the conflicting emotions that welled up inside me at the thought of meeting Stephen Maitland again, the strongest was hatred. True I was frightened, desperately frightened, and I was humiliated too at the way I had been treated, but over and above all this was the recollection of the impression he had made on me in those few brief hours before the nightmare had begun, and for that I couldn't forgive him.

I pulled myself from the restraining hands and said angrily, 'Yes, where is he? Where is Mr High and Mighty Maitland? It's about time he showed his face and his true colours. Or does he always send you two to do his dirty work, all his fetching and carrying, murdering and kidnapping? And for what? What possible, earthly reason . . . '

'Shut up or I'll . . . '

I swung round. 'Shut me up? Oh yes, you'll do that without

a second thought, won't you? But it's too late. I've already talked. Other people know who you are and where you are. Shutting me up will do you no good whatsoever.'

My anger filled me with courage. I felt I could face a den of lions.

'Shut *up*!' said Harvey threateningly, gripping my arm once more.

I took no notice. 'You don't think you can abduct me in broad daylight and get away with it, do you?' Not waiting for a reply I continued with a flourish, 'I was being met at Augsburg this morning by someone who knows all about you. When he finds me missing he'll go straight to the police *and* be able to tell them where I am.'

I stared from one to the other, trembling but triumphant, waiting to see what shattering effect this piece of information would have. It was minimal. Neither of them appeared in the least perturbed and my bravery ebbed away as rapidly as it had arrived. Harvey led me upstairs and opened the door of a small bedroom, pushing me inside. Then he said in a bored voice, 'Save your information for Maitland, it doesn't interest us.'

The door closed behind them and there was the ominous click of a key turning.

The room swam round, and I sat weakly on the edge of the bed, struggling to remain calm. For the first time I was conscious of my shoulder-bag hanging loosely over my arm and I groped inside it, feeling with relief the smooth silver of my cigarette-case. I leaned back against the bed-head, fumbling with my lighter. Dimly I was aware of the freshly-made bed in a room that otherwise bore little signs of occupation. There was a small chest of drawers, a hard-backed chair with a blue and white wash-basin and jug beside it and very little else.

I kicked off my shoes, swinging my feet on to the bed, toying nervously with the strap of my bag. Before I'd had time to collect my thoughts there came the soft pad of feet along the corridor.

I stiffened as they halted, then the door opened abruptly and the Englishman came in. He waved his hand, motioning me to stay where I was, and still without speaking, pulled open the bottom drawer in the tiny chest and withdrew a glass and a bottle of whisky.

He gulped a glassful down then poured another, cupping it in his hands. He said in a completely different manner from that he had used previously: 'You've made a damned mess of things, haven't you?'

The change of tone – the hint of sympathy – was all I needed. I began to cry, oblivious of him, oblivious of everything. He stood silently for a while then sat down on the chair, saying, 'If you don't make less noise, we'll have Ivan for company.'

In front of me the thin curtains at the window wafted gently in the breeze, and the surrounding hills spread into the distance as far as the eye could see, their steep slopes covered with a blanket of fir and pine, an endless vista of rich, verdant green. Above, small wisps of white cloud trailed imperceptibly across the sky. The whole scene was one of peace and tranquillity, disturbed only by the occasional flight of a bird. I wiped my face, abstractedly, wondering at their leaving me alone in a room with an open window, then, remembering the number of stairs we had climbed to reach it, smiled wryly. Unless I wanted to break my neck I was safe enough.

He picked up the bottle again and I turned to look at him. He was sitting, glass in hand, deep in his own thoughts. The air of bad-tempered impatience had gone, and he seemed troubled and anxious. He placed one leg across his knee, lips pursed, gazing into his glass as if therein lay the answer to his problem. The ginger hair was flecked liberally with grey and his skin was flushed and mottled. Looking at him at close range I realized he was older than I had at first supposed. At least fifty, perhaps more. The handle-bar moustache was still immaculately brushed and curled but his tie was loose at the throat and he didn't bother to wipe away the splashes of whisky from the front of his jacket and trousers.

A thread of blue smoke rose slowly to the ceiling and I watched it, hope of escape slowly blossoming. Perhaps, if he was sympathetic to me, perhaps . . .

He twirled his moustache thoughtfully, looking straight at me.

'You've really fouled everything up. Why the hell didn't you leave when I told you to?'

I stared, not understanding. He closed his eyes momentarily, then said through clenched teeth, 'I *phoned* you, for God's sake. If you'd done as I asked . . . '

'You? It was you who phoned? But I thought . . . '

'I told you quite plainly to get out. A child of three couldn't have misunderstood.'

He poured himself another drink and walked over to the window, staring sombrely into the yard below.

'But you'll help me now, won't you?' I said eagerly, clutching the strap of my bag. 'Please, *please* say you'll help me.'

'*Help* you?' He turned round and said in exasperation, 'How the hell can I?' He lowered himself wearily back on to the chair and buried his head in his hands. 'I wish to God I could help you. I didn't bargain for all this. First the girl in Niedernhall, now you . . . '

'That . . . should have been me, shouldn't it?'

He nodded. 'And it wouldn't have been you if you'd kept your nose out of other people's business.' He raised his glass to his lips once more. 'If you hadn't seen me that night . . . '

I said slowly, ' You shouldn't have been out that night, should you? But you had to have a drink . . . '

His face reddened with anger. 'That's none of your business. If you hadn't fancied yourself as a modern-day Mata Hari we'd all be high and dry by now, not chasing all over the countryside for you and your equally stupid friend.'

I gripped my shoulder-bag tightly. Getting angry with him now would do no good at all. With an effort I said calmly, 'Can't we come to some agreement? If you let me go now, right away, you can make it seem it was nothing to do with you. Then you won't have my death on your hands. I promise I won't say anything, anything at all. All I want to do is to go home . . . ' My voice broke and he groaned, the worried frown lines on his brow deepening as he swirled the liquid round in his glass. He said, 'You must understand my position. If anyone found out I'd helped you, my life would be no safer than yours, and when you see the police . . . '

'But I won't! I swear I won't.'

He laughed scornfully. 'Be your age, Miss Carter. Once safely away from here you'll be in the first police station you come to, talking till you're hoarse. Quite honestly, the risk isn't worth it.'

He stood, his decision made. I clenched my fists, my heart beating painfully, afraid to break the silence as he put the bottle and glass back into the drawer. He turned and I closed my eyes. This is it, I thought, as he walked towards me.

He said, 'I'm sorry, lass. Very sorry. But I just can't take the risk of you talking once you get away.'

I looked at him through a blur of tears and fear and said, 'But . . . but surely you only came because you wanted to help me. Surely . . . '

'I came,' he said, looking down at me pityingly, 'because this is the only God-damned place where I've any whisky hidden.'

Through the open window came the sound of footsteps crossing the yard below. He stiffened, then moved swiftly to the edge of the window and peered out from behind the curtain. On seeing whoever it was, he relaxed, letting out a faint sigh of relief.

I licked my lips nervously. 'Is . . . that him?'

He shook his head, staring at me thoughtfully, opened his mouth as if to speak, then, thinking better of it, twirled his moustache and began to pace the room. Four paces one way, four paces another. For several minutes he walked up and down the room in silence, occupied with his own thoughts, then he said abruptly, 'The man you were meeting in Augsburg . . .. were you lovers?'

I gazed at him in astonishment. 'What on earth has that to do with it?'

'*Were* you?'

'No, we were not,' I replied indignantly. 'Though what it has to do with you . . . '

'All right, all right.' He waved a hand deprecatingly and began pacing the room once more. 'I don't mind telling you, young lady, you've made my position intolerable. That girl in Niedernhall . . . ' He shuddered. 'That's not my line, not my line at all.'

'You killed the minister,' I said shortly.

He halted in front of the window, the strong light accentuating the pinched look around his nose and mouth. 'That was different.'

I said bitterly, 'Perhaps you would explain how. If I'm about to die, it's only fair I should know what it's all about.'

'The less you know the better.'

He frowned, obviously deeply troubled, and incredulously I felt sorry for him.

'Keeping me here until Stephen Maitland arrives is only going to make things worse,' I ventured. 'I promise I won't give you away. And if you are caught – and you will be, you know, whether you kill me or not – then if you have helped me, surely that will be in your favour.'

'If I . . . ' He stopped, listening intently. In the distance came the faint sound of a car engine. I saw him tense, then, as the car drew nearer, he made for the door. I jumped up, grabbing his arm, but he pushed me away roughly, saying: 'Don't do anything foolish, understand?' Then the door closed behind him and the key turned, imprisoning me once more.

I ran to the window but the car had drawn to a halt round the side of the house and I could see nothing. Ivan's voice floated across the yard and there was an answering reply but I couldn't make out anything that was said. Like Harvey before me, I began to pace the room, my thoughts in turmoil. The minutes ticked by and I waited expectantly for the sound of approaching footsteps but none came. There was the sound of movement from below my window and I crossed over to it again. Ivan, carrying two large suitcases, was striding towards

93

the corner of the house. He disappeared and then there came the sound of a car boot opening and the cases being heaved in.

I turned despairingly and sat on the bed again, all hope of freedom evaporating. Mechanically I opened my bag, taking out lipstick and powder; if this was to be the finale I was going to look my best. I had just finished running a comb through my hair when there came the unmistakable sound of someone approaching. Hardly able to breathe for the constriction in my chest I rose, facing the door. After an interminable length of time the key turned and the door was flung open by Ivan.

I allowed myself to be led out into the dimness of the corridor, turning without guidance to the left and the head of the stairs. I was aware of dark pictures in gilt frames ranging the breadth of the walls and a large wooden cross hanging on the landing. There was a small round window above it, and shafts of sunlight from the setting sun arrowed down on to the figure of agony nailed below. Instinctively my lips moved in silent prayer, and then we had turned and my hand was sliding down the banister rail as we descended the stairs.

Below us was the entrance hall with its black and white tiled floor. It was empty now and the open door creaked softly on its hinges, swinging gently to and fro. The fragrance from the nearby pine woods hung delicately in the air and a bee buzzed monotonously close by. It was very quiet and still; so still that I could almost believe the house empty save for Ivan and myself. I eyed the distance to the beckoning yard but Ivan's hand closed tightly on my arm, propelling me firmly towards the first of the ground-floor rooms. He gave a sharp knock and then threw the door open, standing behind me as I stood on the threshold.

Chapter Twelve

It was a large room with a high ceiling, criss-crossed by stout beams. Here and there a nail had been hammered in and tankards and brasses hung haphazardly on them. There was a minimum of furniture and, like the room upstairs, it gave the impression of just having had the dust sheets thrown off. Harvey stood before the fireless grate, hands clasped behind his back, eyes carefully averted.

Some yards away from him, framed by the window, stood the man I had been brought to meet. There was a briefcase by his feet and a coat was slung over the chair at his side. He looked as if he wouldn't be detained long by the business in hand. There was a smile on his lips as he gazed at me, rigid and immobile, with Ivan at my back. No one moved. It was as if time hung suspended, and in all the world there were only the four of us. Watching each other. Waiting.

'Surprised, Susan?'

I said slowly, 'I should have known.'

'Yes, you have been rather slow,' he agreed smoothly.

I walked forward a couple of steps to the nearest chair and sat down, feeling like a sleeper who has woken from a long, deep sleep.

'You must have thought it a splendid joke,' I said.

He laughed. 'Yes, if it hadn't been for the inconvenience of it all, it would have been most enjoyable. However, under the circumstances it has become rather trying In fact, you could say this last day or so has been rather a bore.'

'Stephen . . . '

He interrupted me. 'There's no time for recapitulations. Thanks to you, we haven't much time.'

'What do you intend to do with me?' I asked. 'Whatever it

is, you won't get away with it.'

He looked across at me mockingly. 'Because of . . . your friend?'

'Because . . . ' My voice broke and I said stupidly, 'Because men like you never get away with the vile things you do.'

He clapped his hands, applauding. 'You really are too good to be true, Susan. But so wrong.' He lit a cigarette carefully. 'Men like myself *do* get away with whatever they want despite minor . . . problems. Unfortunately you are one such problem and consequently have to be dealt with.'

'And Stephen — have you dealt with him too?'

Gunther stiffened, then moved towards me slowly and threateningly. The mocking smile had disappeared and his eyes were hard and cold. He halted a foot or so away and stared down at me, his mouth a thin line.

'Your knight in shining armour is no longer able to help you. He's rather a headstrong young man who should have minded his own business.' He tapped the ash on his cigarette to the floor. 'He's been more of a nuisance than you, which was quite something. But no longer, I'm glad to say.'

I couldn't help it. It was all suddenly too much. I couldn't keep up the pretence of being unafraid any longer. I began to cry, the tears streaming through my fingers as I covered my face in my hands.

'It may interest you to know that his efforts on your behalf were quite remarkable, especially as I know how . . . un-encouraging you are in personal affairs.'

Behind me Ivan sniggered, but I didn't care. I didn't care about anything but Stephen and my lack of belief in him when all the time it was Gunther who was the villain. Everything was my fault and now it was too late to make amends. *Oh, Stephen. Stephen.*

'And now,' said Gunther, 'we come to you.'

Harvey shuffled his feet and looked nervously at his watch. Ivan too seemed uncomfortable and on edge, but Gunther was as relaxed, as composed, as ever.

'Your car being near the scene of the crash was extremely

fortunate . . . for them. But your actually seeing the men involved . . . that, my dear Susan, was regrettable. For you.'

'But other people must have seen . . . '

'No. The car wasn't missed in Bonn for three hours. By the time the police had put two and two together and realized that Ivan Levos and Harvey Ellis had left the city in it. it was to be safely deposited in the outbuildings at the back. As soon as Levos told me what had happened I drove to the scene of the crash to tow the damn car away. Your presence delayed things, but not too much. As soon as you had gone I brought it here. We are very isolated. I passed no one the whole time.'

'And my car . . . '

'We didn't want *that* on our hands as well, and we most certainly didn't want you reporting its theft to the police, so we returned it. A little dirtier perhaps, but otherwise quite intact.'

'Who shot at me?' I asked bluntly.

He laughed. 'That was Ivan being over-zealous. At that point there was really no necessity to kill either of you. The police hadn't connected the car with the killing, and it looked as if we would all be safely out of the country before they did. However, Ivan is never happier than when out hunting and so . . . ' He shrugged. 'It kept him quiet for a while. Then the next day, with photos of the car all across the front pages of the press, it became a necessity, not only to kill you, but Mr Maitland also.'

'But why Stephen? He hadn't seen them. He couldn't have identified them. He didn't know anything.'

'Not quite true, Susan. He knew enough to come prowling round here asking questions. Harvey caught him when he returned from his unutterably stupid visit to the village, after already ruining things for the sake of a drink. He then thought he had stalled him and let him go.' His voice was heavy with malice and Harvey Ellis flushed angrily, scowling at the carpet, clasping and unclasping his hands behind his back.

'By the time I had returned from my evening out with you and was told what had happened, it was too late.'

97

'Too late?' I echoed.

'Stephen Maitland was nowhere to be found. I went straight after him, but he didn't return to his hotel all night. When I saw the papers in the morning I knew I had to kill you both. Unfortunately I made an error of judgement.'

'And killed Christina instead?'

He raised his eyebrows slightly. 'Yes. A regrettable mistake, but you were a good girl. You rang me to tell me where you were. But there was still no sign of Mr Maitland. When you suggested I travel south with you it seemed a good idea – you couldn't do any harm while I had my eye on you, and it was an excellent way of getting Maitland as well. You were bait, Susan. Nothing but bait. I rang Levos and Ellis from the bar at Schwabisch Hall, telling them what I was doing and to stay put until they heard from me. It worked too. By the time we had reached Nordlingen, there was the little lapdog, frantically searching for his mistress. I left you at the hotel not only to collect my car, but to kill him as well.'

'But he was too clever for you, wasn't he?' I said jubilantly. Viciously.

He struck me across the face. 'Not clever enough, Susan, my dear. Not clever enough. When you rang from Augsburg we had no more time to waste playing games. I decided to lay a false trail, leading Maitland to the Furstenhaus. I sent these men to pick you up, and came back here myself to clear the place of all signs of our stay. Now we split up. After killing you, all I have to do is motor leisurely to the Furstenhaus Hotel in Oberammergau, where without a shadow of doubt the anxious Mr Maitland will be waiting, dispose of him, drive to the airport, and goodbye . . . '

'How are you so sure Stephen will do what you want?'

Gunther smiled, leaning back in his chair steepling his fingers together. 'Harvey Ellis booked you out of the hotel in Augsburg. He said you were moving to the Furstenhaus, Oberammergau, and if there were any queries or post, to forward it there . . . and now . . . ' He lifted the briefcase on to his knee and withdrew two large envelopes, tossing one to

Harvey Ellis and the other to Ivan Levos. The men hastily checked the contents and then Levos said, 'What about the passports?'

Gunther reached into his jacket pocket, pulling out two passports. He handed them to the two men who, money and passports safely stowed away, showed no desire to stay any longer. Gunther rose, adjusting his shirt cuffs with meticulous care.

'You will excuse me, Susan, while I see our friends off the premises.'

Harvey looked up sharply. 'What about you? Aren't you coming as well?'

'A convoy is hardly necessary, Harvey. I'll leave shortly. When the business in hand has been attended to.'

Harvey Ellis looked at me, seemed about to say something, then abruptly turned and the three of them left the room.

I sat quite still, staring into space. From outside came the rise and fall of voices. I heard Stephen's name mentioned and stiffened, straining my ears to catch whatever it was they were saying, but it was no use. The door slammed and I could hear them walking across the yard; this time their voices floated clearly into the room.

'Be sure you split up before Munich Airport.'

'Okay, okay,' replied Harvey Ellis irritably. 'But what about him?'

'Do you think after your performance these last few days I'd leave anything as important as that to you two?'

'I think you're chancing your arm, that's what I think.'

'You've done what you were paid to do. If you've any complaints, you'd better tell me now.' Gunther's voice was harsh and Harvey Ellis didn't reply. The conversation lapsed into German with Ivan Levos sounding as unhappy as Harvey. Then Harvey said as if he could contain himself no longer, 'My letting him go when he came snooping round here wasn't half as bad as you not catching up with him when you knew he was on to us.'

Gunther swore, then said as if talking to a retarded child, 'If

99

I've told you once I've told you a hundred times. His behaviour at Augsburg proves he knows nothing important. He wants to find the girl, that's all. I only missed him by minutes at the hotel. The receptionist said she'd told him Miss Carter had booked out and was travelling to the Furstenhaus Hotel, Oberammergau. That's where he'll be, and that, before the day is over, is where I'll be. There's a flight out in the early morning from Munich. I'll be on it. leaving behind a very harmless Mr Maitland.'

He chuckled. 'Harvey collecting her things and paying her bill was fortunate. We've no problems, none at all.'

I had been so intent on listening to what was being said, that the real point of what I heard passed over me. Suddenly the truth hit me. The room spun round. Stephen was alive after all! Alive and waiting in Oberammergau for me! I gripped the arms of the chair with sweating hands. But he would not be alive much longer if Gunther had his way. Somehow I had to warn him. Somehow. I was dimly aware of Harvey saying, 'I've left my glasses inside, won't be a minute,' and a few seconds later there was the click of the door opening. I ran across to him but before I could implore his help he thrust a key into my palm, saying, 'It fits the front door. Good luck.' Then he was gone.

Seconds later there came the sound of doors slamming and the car which had brought me to the farm lurched on to the dirt track and was away.

Across the yard Gunther's footsteps approached un-hurriedly. I slipped the key into my pocket, bracing myself. Not only my life, but Stephen's, depended on what happened in the next few minutes. For what seemed like an eternity I stood in the centre of the room, watching the door, waiting. When he entered the room he was still smiling, smoothing his blond hair sleekly back, as urbane and unperturbed as ever.

'Alone at last, Susan,' he said softly, closing the door behind him. 'What a pity it has to be in these circumstances. But then, you were never one to avail yourself of opportunities when they arose, were you? We had plenty of

100

time in which to become better acquainted but you played the part of the shy little virgin to perfection and now, alas, it is too late. Unless of course, you have changed your mind?'

'Would it make any difference if I had?'

'Possibly. It would certainly make the afternoon more interesting. Ivan is ringing me when they reach the airport. We have until then before I leave . . . and until your fate is, as they say, sealed.'

'I have a choice then – death or a fate worse than,' I said sarcastically.

'I really believe that is how you would look upon it. I find you quite incredible, Susan. Also amusing, which is why I've taken such risks for you.'

'*Risks!*' I said, genuinely startled. 'What risks have you taken for my sake?'

'Surely they are obvious. I should have killed you that first evening, after Ivan Levos had made such a mess of trying to shoot you in the woods, but instead I waited, thinking that . . . '

'You could amuse yourself with me a little longer, seduce me before the charade was over?'

'Precisely. Unfortunately, of course, the outcome would have been the same. You would have had to die, but that way it would not have been so tiresome.'

'I still fail to see where you've put yourself at risk,' I said, desperately playing for time.

'My dear Susan, if things had gone according to plan, Harvey Ellis would be back in London, Ivan Levos would be continuing his motoring holiday in Alsace-Lorraine, and I would be back home in Brazil. Our success at assassinating Herr Ahlers and getting away with it must be obvious even to a person of your limited intelligence. But not until we have split up and left the country are we truly safe. My delay at tidying up the loose ends, namely you and Mr Maitland, cost us another precious day. This indulging in whims is a failure of mine I must try to control in future.'

He paused, staring at me thoughtfully, the pale blue eyes

revealing nothing. 'It would be a great mistake for your body to be found here,' he said at last. 'I am afraid you must take to the road once more, but this time your journey will be a short one.'

His voice had an air of finality and I knew that, if I was to stall him any longer, I would have to change tactics.

I said softly, 'Is is really necessary? I don't care what you've done with Stephen Maitland, it means nothing to me, but there's really no need to kill me.' I looked across at him meaningfully.

He stubbed out his cigarette and rose, crossing the room towards me, the smile gone.

'So, a fate worse than death is preferable after all?'

'Perhaps your assumptions have been wrong from the start,' I said huskily, the key in my pocket burning like a red hot branding iron. He was in front of me now, his legs brushing against my knees. I took hold of his hand. 'Let's be friends, Gunther,' I begged.

I could tell by the mounting excitement in his eyes that I had struck the right chord. The prospect of making love to me, believing me lulled into a false sense of security, then murdering me, was irresistible. All I had to do was play the game till a chance of using the key arose. Out of the corner of my eye I could see the nose of the Mercedes parked outside. His jacket was still lying over the back of the chair. I didn't know whether his car keys were in the pocket but I could hope. That was all I now had left. Hope.

His voice was thick as he pulled me to him. 'I knew you would see things my way finally.' Then his mouth came down hard on mine, and I closed my eyes, forcing myself to yield. When I could stand it no longer I pushed him away but gently, saying breathlessly, 'We must celebrate.'

His hands were moving expertly over the front of my dress, seeking the buttons, his mouth hot on my throat. I wound my arms around his neck wondering how much longer I could keep this up.

'There's some whisky upstairs,' I murmured. 'Please

102

Gunther, there's a bottle of Scotch in the chest of drawers upstairs. Harvey hid it there.'

He was breathing hard, his eyes glazed. For a horrible, endless moment I thought he was going to refuse.

'Please,' I whispered. 'Don't you want to drink to this occasion?' I stroked his face, fluttering little kisses on his forehead, his eyes.

With a gesture of impatience he put me from him and I could hear him mounting the stairs two at a time. I controlled myself until he had reached the top, then grabbed his jacket. My fingers closed round his key-ring and I raced to the door. Breathless with panic, I struggled with trembling hands to fit the key into the lock. I heard Gunther shout, heard the thud of his feet as he ran along the landing to the head of the stairs, then miraculously the key turned and I was outside.

The constriction in my chest was so tight I thought I was going to faint as the massive door swung shut behind me and I ran to the car, struggling once more with lock and key.

Then I was behind the wheel, manipulating brake and clutch, praying out loud as the running feet drew nearer and nearer. The car lurched off over the uneven cobbles, swerved between the gateposts and skidded on to the rough track that led to freedom.

Like a man demented he ran after me, throwing himself on to the rear of the car. Through the mirror I saw his arms stretched out, struggling to clamber aboard, then he began to lose his grip, fingers clawing at the smooth surface, sliding away inch by inch. I spared him a brief glance as he rolled over and over in the mud, then I hurtled round the bend and down the slope between the dark, beautiful green of the pines.

Chapter Thirteen

The Mercedes shook and swayed down the rough track to the road. With only one thought in mind I swung the wheel hard left, pressing my foot down on the accelerator. I had to reach Oberammergau and Stephen in the shortest time possible.

Darkness had already fallen and the large car felt strange beneath my hands as I speeded recklessly down the narrow, unlit road. I passed the familiar turning to Niedernhall at a suicidal seventy, and then the sudden bend that led on to the main highway south was in front of me. It was too late to slow down. With a prayer on my lips I swerved round it, the car skidding wildly on to the wrong side of the road, the back wheels gouging up the mud and leaves at the roadside. The wheel spun clammily through my hands as I righted the car. Beneath the headlights the road shimmered and gleamed like a live thing, flashing up and under the wheels as the needle on the speedometer hovered between seventy-five and eighty.

I glanced anxiously in the driving mirror for any signs of pursuit, but the road remained blessedly empty. Ahead were a couple of overnight lorries and I dipped my lights, speeding past them down the crown of the road. Eighty . . . eighty-five . . . the Mercedes was like a large bird of prey, eating up all before it as I raced through Schwabisch Hall to Nordlingen.

It was the second time in twenty-four hours that I had travelled this road, but now there was a world of difference. No longer was I chugging along in my old Morris, being led like a lamb to the slaughter. This time I had a powerful car at my disposal . . . and the facts.

All I had to do was keep free of Gunther. I glanced nervously through the driving mirror again, but only the large headlights of the lorries gleamed in the distance. I began to feel more confident. Even if there was another car tucked away at the farm, it wouldn't be as highly powered as the Mercedes, and I knew whereabouts in Oberammergau Stephen would be. The Alte Post. Christina had overheard him making a booking there. For once I held the cards, not Gunther, and Harvey and Ivan would be no use to him now. They would be well on their way to the airport.

At the thought of the airport I froze, my heart in my mouth. To get to Munich they would travel this road. With growing apprehension I tried to remember how far behind them I had been in leaving the farm. Fifteen minutes, twenty? Surely at the speed at which I was travelling I would have passed them by now, and if I had, then they would recognize the car . . .

The road ahead was clear, but through the mirror I could see fresh headlights in the distance and I licked my lips nervously, trying to recall the cars I had passed. Surely if Harvey or Ivan had been at the wheel I would have noticed them? Once again I drove down the narrow, cobbled streets of Nordlingen, past the spot where my Morris had broken down and where, minutes after, Stephen had stood, scanning the crowded street for a glimpse of me. At the thought of Stephen, the tears fell heedlessly down my face. Please God, I prayed. Please let me reach him first. Please let it be all right. Please . . . oh please!

The timbered houses tailed off into fields and vineyards, and the inky blackness of open countryside pressed in on either side of me as I hurtled towards Augsburg, oblivious of everything but the need to reach Stephen.

A hurried glance behind me showed a clear road, and for the first time since I had left the farm, my hands relaxed their grip on the wheel.

I was nearly in Augsburg now. My luck was holding. Once Augsburg was behind me I had nothing to fear from Ivan and Harvey. If they had taken the same road from Niedernhall, then they would turn off it here. Ahead was only Stephen. He was only hours away. Soon my nightmare would be over.

105

My fear had left me now. My intention not to waste a moment in reaching Oberammergau – and Stephen – was calming me. Somewhere, in the dark night behind me, was Gunther. I needed all my wits to escape him. To succumb to the nervous panic that had threatened to overwhelm me earlier would be fatal.

I opened the window slightly, letting some fresh air into the car, trying to think what Gunther's next move would be. His first action after I had left the farm would have been to get hold of a car. To do that, he would have had to ring for a taxi to take him to the village. That could have delayed him anything from fifteen minutes to forty minutes. Then he would have to hire a car . . . With luck I had an hour's start. Without luck . . . I bit my lip. Without luck there would have been another car at the farm. Yet in that case wouldn't he have caught me up by now?

A new, more terrifying thought struck me. Had it all been a little too easy? Was he still using me? Using me to lead him to Stephen? Beads of perspiration broke out on my forehead. I would have to be very careful when I reached Oberammergau. I would have to make it impossible for anyone to follow me to the Alte Post. I slowed down. If I motored into Oberammergau and started knocking up the hotel, I would be pretty conspicuous. If he was behind me . . .

I glanced into the driving mirror, torn by indecision, and a few miles later, where the dark fringe of a wood ran down to the road, I drove the car beneath the trees, bucketing over the rough ground. Tensely I waited in the cold and the dark. Finally I huddled in a corner and fell into a fitful sleep.

Four hours later, stiff and shivering, I drove the car back on to the road, my mouth sour and dry. I became aware of the dark shape of rising ground, of the hills that shelved down to the roadside growing steeper, the tops of the trees, silhouetted in the moonlit sky, growing denser and higher. There was the first subtle lightening of the darkness. In the east the stars had disappeared and the sky was paling to grey. As I watched, the grey became gold and the first fingers of the rising sun appeared beyond the mountains.

Immediately before me the hills remained as an impenetrable black mass across the skyline, but beyond them, bathed in the pale, ghostly light of early morning, were the jagged peaks of the Alps. Like an insurmountable barrier dividing Germany from Austria, they rose, hardening and sharpening as the light grew. Snow glistened on the summits, running like alabaster down the fissures and crevices, and then the countryside around me softened, the darkness turning green as the light increased.

The sun rose and the sky turned a pale, steely blue. On either side of me were soft, undulating grasslands dotted with groups of conifers and small squat bushes. A wooden chalet lay half submerged between one fold of gently rising ground and another, and wild grass grew high at the edge of the road. A soft mist hung over the valley, promising a day of heat and sun.

With growing elation I turned left on the secondary road to Fussen, the ground thick with dew-wet leaves, as I sped through the trees, taking a short cut to Oberammergau. The road dipped and turned, winding beneath giant cliffs to the still sleeping village.

I motored slowly down the main street, searching the hotels and guest-houses for the sign of the Alte Post. The early morning sun shone brightly on the white walls making my tired eyes sting and smart. My head was beginning to throb and I longed for the luxury of clean sheets and a soft bed.

The hotels with their trim wooden fences and scarlet shutters stared back at me, the Gantner, the St. Rochus, the Regentblau. Then, squarely at the end of the street, half hidden by two enormous elm trees, hung the ornate sign of the Alte Post.

Painted saints and angels flanked the door, soaring in an extravaganza of colour around the windows with their troughs of thickly massed flowers, spiralling to the eaves, culminating in a gorgeous riot of cherubim and seraphim. Weak with relief and anticipation, I parked the car and stepped out into the heady mountain air. The little gate swung open with a protesting creak and in the garden birds were singing shrill and sharp. Apprehensively I rang the bell and waited beneath the gently rustling leaves and the protective wings of the painted saints for admittance.

A few minutes later heavy bolts slid back and the door was opened by a stout, red-cheeked woman wearing traditional dress.

I licked my lips nervously. *'Guten Morgen.* Have you a Herr Maitland staying here, please?'

She shrugged. 'Perhaps, Fraulein,'

'Would you check for me, please?'

With a gesture of impatience she turned and I followed her into the sparsely furnished entrance hall. Feverishly I waited while she moved early-morning tea trays from the centre of the reception desk, and then, oh so slowly heaved the guest-book on to the cleared space.

I twisted my head round, trying to see if Stephen's name was on the nearly full page, while she slowly ran her thumb down the list of names.

I said, 'His name is Maitland. Stephen Maitland. He's English.'

'Aaah,' she exclaimed. 'Herr Maitland, room nine.'

Weakly I leaned against the solid oak of the reception desk. 'Could I see him please?' I managed to ask.

She looked at the clock, shaking her head doubtfully.

'It's very important, very . . . '

'At breakfast, Fraulein.'

'I'm Frau Maitland,' I lied desperately. 'I must see him. It's urgent.'

She hesitated, drumming her fingers on the polished wood, then with a slight shrug, picked up the phone. It rang for a few minutes, then Stephen's voice, thick with sleep, answered.

'Good morning, Herr Maitland. Frau Maitland is at reception.'

I couldn't hear his reply. The housekeeper, if that was who she was, replaced the receiver, then settled herself comfortably behind the desk, intent on watching the ensuing reunion with interest. She wasn't disappointed.

Within minutes there came the sound of hurrying footsteps and Stephen burst through the swing doors. I stood stock still, my heart beating painfully against my chest, quite unable to speak. Then I was rushing across the room.

I don't know what I expected his reaction to be. Astonishment, bewilderment, relief. What I didn't expect was for him to hold me away at arms' length and to ask coolly, 'And what are you doing here?'

It was too much. The floor shelved up and I sank to meet it giddily.

When I came to, I was sitting in the only armchair the entrance hall boasted, propped up by Stephen's arm, while the housekeeper stood, face anxious, holding a drink out for me. I accepted it, trying to collect my scattered wits. The housekeeper withdrew to a discreet distance and Stephen removed his arm, asking once more, 'Why are you here?'

'I'm here,' I said, with as much dignity as the situation allowed, 'because Gunther Cliburn is going to kill you.'

He said simply, 'Is he indeed, and what is that to you?'

'What is that to me?' I echoed. 'Sweet heaven, I drive like a maniac all the way down here to warn you, instead of doing what anyone in their right minds would do, and drive to the nearest Channel port and home, and all you can do is ask me why I've bothered.'

Stephen sat on the edge of the coffee table in front of me, his whole attitude one of cool indifference.

'Before I believe anything you say, I think I'm owed an explanation.'

I said, 'I can explain to you, Stephen, but it will take time, and Gunther must be searching the hotels already.'

'Then it might be a good idea to move the car.'

'Oh goodness, I'd forgotten all about it.' The familiar stirrings of panic rose within me.

'Go up to my room,' he said. 'I'll garage the car and then we'll have our talk. I warn you. Your explanation had better

109

be good. I'm still seven hundred pounds' worth of car missing.'

I handed him the keys and he strode out on to the veranda, his face an impenetrable mask. Obediently I staggered off in search of room nine. It was on the ground floor at the back of the hotel. It was small, containing only a single bed and chest of drawers. The walls were stark white and over the head of the bed hung an ornate crucifix. French windows opened on to the stretch of green beyond and I walked over to them, opening them and standing on the dew-wet grass. I didn't turn when the door behind me opened and then closed quietly.

He came to stand a foot or two away from me before he spoke. 'Why did you do it?' he asked then. I turned and walked back into the room.

'You mean at Nordlingen?'

He nodded.

'I thought you were going to kill me.'

He drew in his breath and said with barely controlled anger, 'You'll have to think of something better than *that*!'

'It's the *truth,*' I shouted back, my control snapping like an over-taut thread. 'For goodness sake, listen to me, will you?'

We glared at each other, then he said, 'Okay, I'm listening.'

I stared at the floor and said, 'It was all your fault. You lied to me. That first evening after we had visited the church in the woods, I went out for a walk. I recognized Harvey Ellis leaving the wine bar in Niedernhall. I was so sure it was the same man who had stolen my car that I followed him. He went to the farm and, when I got there, I saw your car parked in the woods *and* I saw you talking to him.

'When I met Gunther later, he said you had left a message for me, that you would be late in the morning because you had gone to Koblenz. I didn't think too much of it then because I was sure you would explain everything to me when you saw me. But the next day I read in the papers about Herr Ahlers being shot in Bonn and saw the photograph of the car and realized that the two men who had crashed it and taken mine were the killers.'

I twisted my signet ring round and round my little finger.

'There were no descriptions of the wanted men in the paper. I knew, then, that the shot in the woods had not been an accident. Someone knew I had seen the men and that I could identify them. My first thought was to ring you but I didn't have your number and I didn't know the name of the guest-house, but I did have Gunther's telephone number.

'So I rang him. It was he who first made me suspicious of you. He pointed out that you had been travelling behind the car the men had crashed and when I told him that I'd seen you talking to one of them at the farmhouse when you had said you were in Koblenz, well . . . it did seem odd but I was still sure you would be able to explain everything when I saw you. Really I did. But when you came you held to your story about Koblenz, and later, when you went to the chemist for me . . . I found the gun in your glove compartment.'

Stephen swore under his breath.

'I . . . thought Gunther was right,' I went on. 'After all a pistol isn't standard holiday equipment, is it? When I got back to Frau Schmidt's there was an anonymous telephone call for me, telling me to leave Niedernhall immediately. I couldn't recognize the voice but he did speak English, so I put two and two together . . . '

I sat down on the edge of the bed, still not raising my eyes to his face.

'Before I left I went for a coffee and a sandwich. I saw Christina across the street and waved to her to join me. She told me you were leaving Ohringen and gave me the name of the hotel you'd booked in at at Oberammergau. Her father had dropped her off so that she could do some shopping and return my scarf which I had left at their guest-house.' I paused, struggling to steady my voice. 'I told her to keep it. That's why . . . that's why she was killed. She was wearing it and they . . . they thought it was me.'

Stephen swore under his breath.

'I was terrified. I knew whoever had done it would soon realize their mistake, and the only person I could think of who had seen me wearing the scarf was you. I drove straight out of

111

the village and phoned Gunther. He came to meet me and he said . . . he said you and the two men who had taken my car had all been arrested. All I wanted to do was to drive out of that village and never see it again. I told Gunther I was going to Austria and he said he would travel with me as far as Augsburg.

'You see, they didn't know where you were and they thought by using me as bait they would get you as well. When we reached Nordlingen my car broke down. Gunther took it to be repaired and it was then that I saw you. You passed me in the street and I saw you park behind Gunther's Mercedes and get out of the car.'

I groaned, covering my head in my hands. 'I ran in search of Gunther. He made a pretence of telephoning the police, but in actual fact he phoned the two men -- Ivan Levos and Harvey Ellis -- and then booked us both into the hotel on the outskirts of the town. After dinner he took a cab and went back to Nordlingen for his car, and not long after I saw you climbing the hill, and I thought . . . ' The tears began to fall despite myself. 'I thought . . . you . . . were going to kill me, so I ran . . . '

'And took my car?'

'Yes, I drove to Augsburg and booked into a hotel there. I rang Gunther to let him know where I was and of course he sent Harvey Ellis and Ivan Levos to pick me up. The joke had worn thin as far as he was concerned. I went to buy a morning paper and they kidnapped me in the street. Just like that. When I came round we were well on our way back to Niedernhall . . . I still thought it was you who was trying to kill me. They encouraged me in that, saying you were at the farmhouse waiting for me. Of course it was Gunther all along. He was . . . vile.'

'Did he touch you?' Stephen asked.

I bit my lip, eyes shut tight against a fresh onslaught of tears.

I heard Stephen say quietly, 'So help me, I'll break every bone in his body.'

And then I looked up and saw his face, harsh and haggard, and I knew that everything, at least where he and I were concerned, was all right. He pulled me roughly into his arms and kissed me hungrily. It was a long time before he let me go.

I looked up at him and said shakily, 'I'm sorry I was such a fool, Stephen.'

He pressed my head against his shoulder, winding his fingers in my hair.

'I was the fool, Susan. I should have levelled with you from the beginning, but I wasn't sure of things and I didn't want to frighten you.'

'But you'll tell me now?'

'Of course. Where shall I begin?'

'With the gun,' I said.

Chapter Fourteen

He put his arm around me, holding me close. 'I was probably more scared of that damned gun than you were.'

'But why did you have it?'

He grinned. 'At the time I wasn't sure myself. The ironic thing is, I never realized about the car. I haven't read a damned paper since I left Munich. It was other things that disturbed me. You remember when we went to Ohringen for a couple of drinks?'

'And Christina sent me for the booklet so that she could speak to you in private?'

'Exactly. Anyway that was what started it off. She'd told her father about Herr Cliburn and he was sure there was no one of that name and description staying in Niedernhall.'

'I remember that, but why . . . '

'Don't interrupt,' he said, closing my lips with a kiss. 'Well, like you, I didn't think any more of it until that incident in the woods, and that, my love, was just *too* much. As you pointed out yourself, you don't use a silencer if you're potting a rabbit. Whoever fired that shot had been aiming it carefully. The shot was fired from the top of the ridge *down* on to the clearing where you were sitting. It couldn't have been an accident.'

'You mean you knew then that someone had tried to kill me and didn't *say* anything!'

'What good would it have done? You would only have been scared silly. It was obvious from your behaviour that you didn't know what was happening. I decided I'd better make it my business to know, and I started off with Herr Cliburn. No one had heard of him. Then I rang Christina. She said her father was quite firm about there not being a resident of the

114

village with that name, and that he wasn't one of the regulars who spend part of the summer here. It was Christina who suggested the farm. Apparently it's often let during the summer months.'

'So you went up to find out?'

'Yes. My car didn't take very kindly to that dirt track, so I left it half-way up and walked the rest of the way. I was still about twenty yards away when your friend careered out of the woods, nearly running me down. He was in a foul temper and had been drinking heavily. It soon developed into quite a slanging match. He said he didn't like strangers nosing around his property and that there was no one of the name of Cliburn staying there and to beat it. But one thing I did get a nosy at was his car, and on the back seat was a rifle.'

'If it had been Ivan Levos you had spoken to and not Harvey Ellis, he would have killed you there and then.'

'He may have tried,' Stephen said dryly. 'Anyhow, I'd seen enough to make me uneasy. Cars don't get stolen and then returned with such a minimum of fuss. And people don't get as excited as Ellis did over a harmless trespasser. I was pretty sure the rifle in his car wasn't coincidence and I decided that the first thing to do was to get you out of Niedernhall.'

'So . . . '

'So I went to Koblenz.' He pressed his fingers gently against my lips to silence my next question. '*Because* it just so happens I have an old school friend, Paul Beincen, living there, who not only speaks English on account of having an English mother, but is also a police officer.'

'Oh, so you told him and he . . . '

'Not so fast, Susan. He wasn't at home. His sister was there and gave me dinner, but Paul was away for two weeks on a training course.'

'So it was a wasted journey?'

'Not quite,' he said, with a sheepish grin. 'I borrowed his gun.'

'You did *what*!' I cried, jumping to my feet. 'You took a gun belonging to a German police officer! Stephen, do you

115

realize what could happen to you, they could . . . '

'Ssssh, don't get so excited. He won't miss it until he gets back, and after all, it did seem as if I might need it . . . '

'But, Stephen, you wouldn't actually have *used* it, would you?'

'Not unless I had to.'

'Stephen . . . '

'I booked us into this hotel, the Alte Post, though *not*, I may add, as Frau Maitland, and after you'd agreed to come with me, went back to Ohringen to collect my things and try and get in touch with Paul again. Then I heard about Christina, and the way she'd died. I drove over to Niedernhall like a madman but it was too late. You'd gone. The ironic thing is, I never realized about the car, I never saw the papers. If I'd had proof like that I would have been in the first police station.'

'How did you trace me as far as Nordlingen?'

'Luck mainly. Among the people standing outside Frau Schmidt's was the man who had served you in the coffee-bar. I was asking everyone if they had seen you or your car, and he had. He said you'd taken the Schwabisch Hall road. I hared off after you but without success. I drove through Schwabisch Hall and as far as Crailsheim before I gave up. Then I doubled back to Schwabisch Hall and began a tour of the streets.'

'And the bars.'

'Eventually.' He grinned. 'That *really* put the cat among the pigeons. The barman remembered you very well. He gave me a most glowing account of your rapturous reunion with his fellow countryman. He probably thought, by my behaviour, that I was an outraged husband, and he really went to town.'

I blushed shamefacedly. 'It was just that I'd been so frightened and . . . '

He silenced me in mock reproach. 'Never mind the excuses. You've a lot to answer for, young lady. What he said really took the wind out of my sails, I can tell you. I didn't know what to make of it. The barman had seen you studying a map and had overheard Gunther mention Augsburg. So, like Alice, muttering curioser and curioser, I headed as fast as I could in the same direction.'

'Until you got to Nordlingen and saw Gunther's car.'

'I waited by that damned car for over an hour. Then I did what was becoming routine. Rang all the hotels and guest-houses and finally traced you about eight o'clock.'

'What made you hide the car and walk up to the hotel?'

'I'm not sure. Some sixth sense that I wish I'd never heeded! I asked for you at Reception and was told that Fraulein Carter was not receiving visitors. When I insisted, I was told that I must wait and see her Doctor, Herr Cliburn, who had gone to Nordlingen for medical supplies. That did it. I was sure then that you were being held against your will. I was just making my way to the back of the hotel to see if I could force an entrance when I saw you running and jumping down the hillside like a maniac. It never occurred to me that you were running away from *me*. How I didn't break a leg chasing after you I'll never know. Then, when you did see me, instead of running gratefully into my arms, you ran even harder and stole my car!'

'I'm sorry, Stephen. Really I am.'

He shook his head. 'I sat down on the edge of that road, trying to decide who was mad, you or myself.'

I squeezed his hand. 'The hotel staff definitely thought it was me, by the way they behaved. I'd seen your torch bobbing about, getting nearer and nearer and when I was sure it was you I dashed to the reception desk to ask them to phone the police, with the result that I found myself being firmly taken to my room and very nearly locked in.'

Stephen laughed. 'My poor Susan. How did you convince them of your sanity?'

'I didn't. But when they'd gone back downstairs I sneaked out by a rear exit.'

'And drove straight to Augsburg?'

'Yes. What did you do, Stephen? Hire another car?'

'I walked back to Nordlingen, booked into a hotel and spent the most wretched night of my life trying to reason things out. Next morning I rang the hotel on the off chance you had returned. You hadn't, but this time they were helpful. They said Fraulein Carter had booked out of the hotel and gone to the St Wolfgang, Augsburg.'

'But how did they know that?'

'When you phoned Gunther from Augsburg, he obviously made his mind up there and then as to how he would deal with us both. He sent Ellis and Levos to pick you up early next morning and take you back to the farm, and left a clear trail for me to follow, from Augsburg to Oberammergau. That way, Gunther would know just where I was when he had settled with Ellis and Levos and murdered you. All he had to do was catch up with me here on his way to Munich and a flight back to Brazil. Most convenient for him.'

'Except that I got away and you didn't go to the Furstenhaus.'

'No. As I'd already got a booking here I stuck to it.'

'I'm glad.'

He kissed me again and I was too happy to feel any fear at the thought of Gunther. I said, 'What are you going to do now? Ring the police?'

'Yes. I'd better not waste any more time.'

He squeezed my shoulder. 'I'll phone from the reception desk. The manageress speaks reasonable English and I may need someone to help me out.'

'I'll come with you. I can get a coffee while you're phoning.'

Hand in hand we walked down the corridor and into the hall. The manageress smiled, pleased with our reconciliation. I left Stephen to explain things to her and went in search of the dining-room. It was eight o'clock now and all six tables were taken. I paused, trying to estimate if anyone was about to leave, but the chattering couples and families showed no sign of moving. A waiter approached anxiously, and asked if I could wait a half hour or so.

'*Nein*,' I replied. 'I only want a coffee, nothing else. Please don't bother.'

Through the picture windows I had a clear view of the

street. There was no sign of Gunther Cliburn. Across the narrow road was a village shop selling souvenirs, sweets and newspapers. I hesitated and then went back to the reception desk.

Stephen seemed to be doing quite well. The manageress was following his conversation with open-mouthed amazement. I breathed a sigh of relief. It was nearly over. Ahead of us were some hours of police questioning, but it was nearly over, and I was safe and Stephen was safe.

Across the street I could see the headlines of the papers and recognized the name of Herr Ahlers. I gazed searchingly up and down but there were only tourists and villagers. Opening my bag I took out the marks I needed for the paper, then ran quickly down the short path to the gate, and sprinted across the street.

It was a beautiful day. In front of me, rising sheer above the whitewashed walls of chalets and hotels, was a precipitous wall of rock. A giant crag jutted menacingly above the village, its silver-grey face devoid of the grass and trees that clothed the lower slopes. I shivered, averting my eyes to the lush meadows, thick with summer flowers of white and yellow, and to the flamboyant religious frescoes that decorated the walls of the houses lining the street.

The doorway of the little shop was jammed with camera-slung tourists. I squeezed round a generously-built American woman in red gingham and took a newspaper from the rack. The only photographs on the front page were of Herr Ahlers and his widow and family. With difficulty I managed to open the centre page and had a glimpse of the car before the press of people jostling me forced me to close it.

'Sorry, honey, was that your foot?' It was the American woman.

'It's all right,' I assured her, trying to reach the counter.

'Why, Hamilton. Just you come here a minute. The young lady here is English! You are English, honey, aren't you?'

I nodded.

'I knew it. I just knew it! Why, we've just this minute left

119

England. What a lovely country that is! Hamilton and I just fell in love with it, didn't we, honey? We spent two whole days in Edinburgh and two in Stratford-upon-Avon where your great poet was born, and three days in London looking at all the sights. Do you come from London, Miss . . . '

'Carter. Susan Carter.' I said, trying to catch the eye of the young boy behind the counter.

'Well, we surely are pleased to meet you, Miss Carter. I'm Myrtle Bosemann and this is my husband, Hamilton.'

An equally large American with a beaming smile and a flowered shirt shook my hand enthusiastically.

'Pleased to meet you, Miss Carter. My wife and I have just been looking at your lovely country and it sure was a mighty wrench to leave it. Though I must say this here little place is pretty fine. Kinda like a kiddies' toy-town.'

My money for the paper was finally taken from my outstretched hand, but by this time I was wedged firmly between Mrs Bosemann's ample bosom and her husband, who seemed genuinely pleased to see me and loath to let me go.

'Have you been here long, Miss Carter?'

I shook my head. 'I arrived this morning.'

'Is that so? Well now, Mrs Bosemann and I would just love to show you around, wouldn't we, honey?'

Mrs Bosemann nodded vigorously.

'We saw the darndest place yesterday, built by mad King Ludwig of Bavaria. That place really takes some beating. We'd think it an honour to take you round there this morning. The tours set off from the square in fifteen minutes from now. Look, you can see the coaches from here.' He pointed down the street. 'I know Mrs Bosemann would just love to see it again. When you get there you can hire little horse-drawn traps and drive right up the mountain to the castle and . . . '

'Oh, you'd just love it, honey,' interrupted Mrs Bosemann. 'This King Ludwig was just mesmerized by Wagner, so much so that he imagined himself to be the knight of the swan in Wagner's opera. Isn't that the wildest thing? He even had armour made for himself, and this castle, Neuschwanstein, was built by him as a theatrical setting for his delusions.'

'Myrtle reads *all* the tourist guides,' her husband said proudly.

'I've got what they call a photographic memory, honey. Do you know, the King thought the castle was the castle of the Holy Grail and . . . '

'Thank you very much,' I managed at last. 'It really is most kind of you, but I'm afraid I can't. I must go now.' I edged away. 'I do hope you enjoy the rest of your holiday.'

'Aw, honey, I was so looking forward to it.' Mrs Bosemann's face fell. 'Hamilton and I just love company and I'm sure you would have enjoyed it.'

I squeezed her hand. 'It was lovely of you to ask me, really it was, but I'm with someone you see, and . . . '

'That's all right, honey. I understand. But mind you see that crazy castle. It's only about thirty miles away and, like Hamilton said, it really is the darndest place.'

'I will, and thank you for the thought.'

I turned away quickly, touched by their unaffected kindness.

Tucking the paper securely under my arm, I emerged into dappled sunlight and began to walk the few yards down the street to the point opposite the Alte Post. The sun seemed palpably hotter with every passing minute and I hoped that the police questioning which lay before us would not last too long. A wasp zoomed uncomfortably near my ear and I turned my head sharply. It was then that I saw the fair-haired figure step back hurriedly into a doorway.

Suddenly I was ice-cold, caught once more in the familiar grasp of barely controlled panic. The blood pounded in my ears as I gazed unseeingly into the nearest shop-window. Slowly I raised my eyes and looked back once more along the street.

A crowd of teenagers, barefoot and wearing pale blue jeans and strings of hippy beads, sauntered noisily past me, followed by a stern-faced woman with two solemn children in tow. I hesitated, then, instead of crossing the street to the hotel, I

121

strolled on, stopping now and then to gaze into shop-windows, furtively trying to see if any of the blond heads bobbing backwards and forwards in the village street belonged to Gunther. There was no sign of him. I paused, my heart hammering slightly less painfully.

I was jumping at shadows. My nerves were so over-wrought that I was imagining things. Breathing easier, I wiped the perspiration from my forehead and smiled shakily at my reflection.

There was a full-length mirror running on the left-hand side of the window, which made the shop, packed with lavishly-embroidered blouses and velvet waistcoats, seem twice as large. It also reflected very clearly the people in the street behind me. As I looked past my own reflection I saw Gunther step cautiously out of his doorway, then, seeing I had come to a halt, draw back quickly.

'Oh God, *no*!' I clenched my nails into my palms so tightly that I drew blood. My head was spinning.

Gunther was waiting for me to lead him to Stephen. He would make no attempt on my life until I'd done that. I licked my lips nervously. He must have raced to the Furstenhaus Hotel in an effort to catch me up before I could see Stephen and we could inform the police. What must he have thought when he reached it to find neither of us there? That Stephen hadn't swallowed the bait and was staying in a different hotel from the one he had been led to believe I was at? That I was now doing the rounds and searching for him? That as yet I still hadn't found him and still hadn't seen the police?

I stood in an agony of indecision. Should I dash back to the Alte Post and hope that the police would arrive before Gunther acted. That he would act, and act immediately, I didn't doubt. After all, he had nothing to lose.

A family with four children stepped out of the hotel. The parents seated themselves at one of the wrought-iron tables in the hotel's garden while the children played noisily, chasing each other round the chestnut trees, laughing and screaming excitedly.

I couldn't take the risk of leading Gunther inside the Alte Post among defenceless people. Or among the not so defenceless come to that. The thought of Stephen's borrowed gun set a fresh ripple of fear down my spine: the risks were too great. Stephen must be warned. He had to be able to tell the police, so that they could arrest Gunther without danger to anyone else. But how?

Like the United States cavalry riding to the rescue, I saw Mrs Bosemann bearing her royal way down the narrow pavement, beaming expansively at everybody she passed, delighted with Bavaria, delighted with Mr Bosemann, delighted with life in general. Like a ship in full sail she swept down on me.

'Susan Carter! Are you going to buy one of those blouses? They really are the nicest things. Hamilton, don't you think one of those blouses would suit Susan fine?'

'Sure it would, honey. Why, you'd look pretty as a picture in one of those and a fancy waistcoat to match.'

I stepped into the doorway, out of sight of watching eyes, fumbling in my bag for pen and paper, my mind made up. Mrs Bosemann had said the coaches left for Neuschwanstein at ten-fifteen. That's where I would lead Gunther.

'Could you do me a favour, Mrs Bosemann? Could you take this message to Stephen Maitland in the hotel opposite?'

'Why sure, honey. But what's the matter? Don't you feel well?'

'I'm all right, it's just that . . . ' I gazed into her puzzled blue eyes. 'It's just that . . . '

'Is Mr Maitland the friend you were telling us about?'

I nodded. The blue eyes cleared. 'I understand, honey. You young people have had a quarrel.'

I nodded again.

'Well now, if we can help in any way we'll be glad to. I know what it's like when you fall out and then regret it. Pride can be a very painful thing. Why I remember not talking to Hamilton for a whole week when we were courting. Isn't that right, honey?'

123

Mr Bosemann nodded. 'You just give us your *billet doux* and we'll pop across the road with it. No bother at all, Miss Carter. And if you and Mr Maitland would like to accompany us this afternoon . . . '

'Hamilton!' Mrs Bosemann exclaimed, prodding him vigorously. 'If they've just quarrelled, they'll want to make things up, and they won't want us around for *that*.'

Mr Bosemann grinned sheepishly. 'I guess that's so. Just the same, I reckon it would be a good idea to give Miss Carter the name of our hotel. Don't you think so, Myrtle?'

'I most certainly do. There now. Have you finished your note?'

She slipped it into her handbag. 'Don't you worry another minute. Hamilton and I are going straight over there. And you give us a ring and let us know how things are. Here's the name and number of our hotel. We're here till Friday. And don't you worry. Everything's going to be all right.'

Wishing I could be as sure of that as she was, I stepped out of the shadowed doorway and began to walk briskly down the street, away from the hotel. I didn't bother to scan the windows in order to catch a glimpse of Gunther. I knew he was behind me. Miraculously my fear had left me. I felt quite calm. Even buoyant. Mrs Bosemann had saved the day. In my hurried note I had written:

Gunther is following me. Am making for Neuschwanstein on a guided tour. He won't harm me till I've led him to you. If you ring the police they should be able to pick him up when the tour buses reach the castle. Lovingly, Susan.

This time it was I who was setting the trap and Gunther who was walking into it. If Neuschwanstein was thirty miles away, as Mrs Bosemann had said, then it would take a good thirty minutes, perhaps longer, depending on the state of the roads, for the coaches to reach the castle. When they did so, Gunther would step straight into the arms of the law.

The street broadened into a cobbled square, spoiled by the giant super de luxe coaches waiting to take tourists to the twin castles of Neuschwanstein and Hohenschwangau. They were more than half full already. The drivers were standing beside giant blackboards advertising their destinations, loudly extolling in French, German and English the delights in store for those who took the trip.

I smiled grimly to myself, imagining Gunther's perplexity when he saw me mount the nearest coach. This would have him well and truly foxed. The driver took my money and gave me my ticket without pausing for breath as he harangued the tourists passing by to 'join me in a tour of the fairytale castles of King Ludwig of Bavaria.'

At the rear of the coach were a group of barefoot teenagers who had passed me earlier. I edged in front of them into a corner seat, settling myself comfortably with the pamphlets I had received with my ticket. That Gunther was also safely esconced in another coach I didn't doubt. Whether he was also reading his pamphlets was another matter.

Chapter Fifteen

I kept my head bent, to all outward appearances intent on the booklets on my knees. The Bosemanns would have handed my note to Stephen and by this time he would have telephoned the police. I glanced surreptitiously across the square in the direction of the Alte Post, but there was no sign of Stephen, and none of Myrtle and Hamilton Bosemann. I felt a flicker of unease, wondering for the first time if what I was doing was sensible. Yet what alternative had I had? To have led Gunther Cliburn into the hotel without giving Stephen any warning would have been madness. This way was surely safer and easier, and yet . . .

I bit my lip. Gunther was no fool. Wouldn't he think it odd, this trip I was making to Neuschwanstein? Why should I be looking for Stephen there? I pressed my arms across my stomach, trying to suppress the growing anxiety I felt. After all, I tried to convince myself, whether he thought it odd or not didn't really matter. All that mattered was that he follow me. I was quite safe. It wouldn't even be necessary for me to leave the coach. When we arrived, the police would be there and that would be that. I wondered if Stephen, too, would be there, and hoped with passionate intensity that he would.

The coach driver shouted his wares once more, then jumped aboard the coach.

To the left of us, an engine throbbed into life and a coach eased past. Our driver pushed open the window in the roof above his head, and began to follow. There were still three more coaches to the right of us. The desire to crane my head round, searching for Gunther was nearly too much. With difficulty I kept my eyes lowered, leafing unseeingly through the pamphlets. He would be on one of them. He wouldn't let

126

me get away from him again.

Gathering speed, the coaches slipped out of Oberammergau and headed towards the mountains. I leaned back, relaxing slightly, soothed by the rhythmic sway of the coach as it left the village and sped down the country road. Behind me, the teenagers chattered gaily in French, undisturbed by the disapproving glances given them by the properly dressed German tourists across the aisle.

At either side the road was bounded by green meadows and flowers. Behind them rose the hills, dotted with copses of fir and spruce, with an occasional cluster of low-lying chalets surrounding an onion-domed church. Then the trees, slope after slope of them, their rich greenery like a dark shadow encircling the base of the mountains. The silver-grey cliffs and precipices pierced the blue sky, the sun shining brilliantly on the snow-capped peaks and the snow-filled fissures and ravines. It was breathtaking, and despite the circumstances, I felt my heart leap with pleasure as we drew nearer, climbing gradually higher. The trees grew thicker, pressing in on either side, and the heady smell of the pines permeated the coach as we wound our way through the woods. In the distance I caught a glimpse of a turret and a slender spire and a flash of blue water, then they were gone and there was only the leafy dimness of the trees and the narrow road deep in pine needles. Shafts of sunlight pierced the branches, glistening on the ferns and bracken, catching the shimmering tip of a bird's wing as it darted in and out of the shade. Everything had a lustre, was peaceful, calm.

No discreet cars had overtaken us as I had expected, though the road was so narrow that it would have been difficult for anything to pass. The realization brought relief. The sight of police cars or anything remotely similar would put Gunther on his guard. They would stay behind the coaches until we arrived. The German police weren't scatter-brained even if I was. Nothing could go wrong. Not this time. Stephen wouldn't let it.

'*Voudriez-vous en?*'

I turned with a start. One of the French girls held out a bag of sweets.

I smiled. '*Merci.*'

'You are English?'

I nodded. She laughed delightedly. '*Bon.* We were having a little bet. My friends, they thought you were *Américaine,* but I said you were *Anglaise.*'

They hung over the back of the seat, laughing and chattering noisily.

'You were all alone, so . . . ' She shrugged, flicking her hair back over her shoulder. 'If you wish, come with us.'

The others nodded in agreement. I shook my head.

'There is no need to be shy!' she exclaimed, the shiny lips parted in a wide smile. 'This is Michel.'

A blond-haired boy with a beard gave a mock bow.

'And Pierre.'

'*Enchanté, m'selle.*'

'And Roland and Catherine.'

They shook my hand enthusiastically.

'We are quite safe, *très respectable*!' She looked down her nose, giving a very good impression of the woman sitting across the aisle. '*Je suis Annabelle.*'

'Well, thank you very much, Annabelle, but I don't think I'll be going round the castle.'

'*Alors*! Not see the castle! Then why . . . '

I laughed. 'It's a long story, too long to tell. Thank you, all the same.'

She pouted prettily. 'Roland will die of love, if you do not.'

Roland blushed furiously while the others laughed.

'That is true.' Pierre put an arm around his friend in mock comfort. 'For Roland's sake, you must join us at the castle.'

Roland pushed him away good-humouredly. 'Take no notice, they are children . . . '

He looked all of sixteen. 'My name is Roland Dupré, and I have to suffer these . . . these — *imbéciles.*'

The others shrieked with laughter.

'Your name, mademoiselle?'

128

'Susan. Susan Carter.'

'You will join us?'

I shook my head amid loud protestations.

'I am meeting somebody — at least I hope to. In any case I shall not be staying.'

'But if he is not there, you will have to wait until the coaches return,' said Annabelle.

I shook my head once more.

'We will make you change your mind. Look! We are almost there.'

Roland pointed through the window. Ahead of us the road widened, curving its way out of the trees into a large clearing that was used as a car park. The woods enclosed three sides, but to the north lay a glistening, shimmering sheet of water.

'Oh!' exclaimed Annabelle. '*Magnifique*!'

The deep, aquamarine lake lay resplendently girdled by the pine-covered hills that swept down to its banks, the soaring mountains casting brilliant reflections on to the still, shining surface. I caught my breath. Annabelle was right. It was magnificent.

The coach we had been following had already drawn to a halt and passengers were climbing out, standing in little groups, admiring the view. As our coach pulled round, I could see the one behind emerge from the woods. I found I was holding my breath and my hands, gripping my shoulder-bag, were clammy. This was it. This was the end. All I had to do was stay put.

Annabelle's hand rested lightly on my shoulder. 'Come . . . '

'No, really, Annabelle.'

She stared down at me for a moment, then shrugged. 'If that is what you wish . . . '

I wished I could explain. Seeing that I meant it and wasn't going to join them, they all waved goodbye and noisily stepped into the bright sunshine. As the other passengers collected their bags and cameras and filed down the coach steps I remained in my seat, watching.

The remaining two coaches swept round in a large arc,

halting at the far side of the clearing. I waited expectantly. There was nothing. No cars behind them. No men in uniform. Nothing. Only the sun beating down on to the dusty ground, and the glittering, silent surface of the lake beyond. I felt sick, my stomach contracting painfully, my throat tightening till I could hardly swallow.

'*Please, God. Please*!'

Gunther stepped out of the last coach. Like a cornered animal I watched mesmerized as he strolled behind the other tourists, as his eyes lifted slowly towards me, smiling with cold triumph as I huddled, terrified, in the corner of the deserted coach.

It was no use. It had never been any use. One glance at him, arrogant and self-assured, had been enough to convince me of that. I began to gather things together. The pamphlets, my shoulder-bag, the sweets that Annabelle had given me. As I did so, I saw the driver of Gunther's coach leap down from his seat, and ignoring the throng of passengers grouped round the coach's open doorway, make straight for Gunther.

I stiffened, watching with bated breath as the driver planted himself firmly in front of Gunther. I could see the expression on Gunther's face change from one of displeasure to one of annoyance and then anger. He stepped to one side but the driver grabbed his arm, shouting loudly for his ticket. Within minutes, the two of them were surrounded by interested tourists and all that was visible were the driver's waving arms.

I didn't wait to see the outcome. Tugging open the door of the coach I raced across the car park in the direction the other passengers had taken. If I could catch up with Annabelle and her friends they would help me. By the time I had explained to anyone else, Gunther would be free of the irate driver and it would be too late.

I plunged into the trees and up the narrow path that led towards the castle. As I rounded the first bend I recognized the other occupants of the coach strolling along unconcernedly some yards ahead. I pushed my way through them, running as fast as I could over the loose gravel. The track widened, and beneath the trees was a small chalet where souvenirs and postcards, sweets and candyfloss, were sold.

Frantically I scanned the interior, but of Annabelle and her friends there was no sign. I looked around me, feeling my self-control slipping away. I hadn't passed them and they weren't in the shop and ahead of me, on the road leading to Neuschwanstein, were only a party of scouts and an elderly couple.

A few yards away was a queue of horse-drawn landaus, waiting to take tourists who felt that the steep climb to the castle was too much for them. As I watched, the sour-faced woman, who had sat across the aisle from me in the coach, drove off in the first one. The rest of the coach party, in twos and threes, reached the carriages and began climbing inside. No one it seemed was going on foot. Breathlessly I ran across, shouting at the first driver.

'Have some teenagers just hired a carriage?'

He flicked the reins and the horse began to move obediently forwards. I grabbed hold of the harness.

'Please. It's very important!. Three boys and a girl. Have they just hired a carriage to the castle?'

Irritatedly he pulled up.

'The carriage only holds four people, Fraulein, and it is full. Now, if you will excuse me . . . '

'I don't want to hire it. I just want to know if you have seen three boys and a girl and if they took a landau up to the castle. Please, it's very urgent. Have you seen them?'

He frowned, rubbing his mouth with the back of his hand. 'Perhaps. Many people use the carriages. It is a long walk, especially in the sun.'

'But in these last five minutes!' I cried desperately.

He stared at me, his eyes blank. My heart was hammering painfully in my chest, and each approaching footstep was stretching my over-taut nerves to breaking point. I gripped the reins tightly. 'The carriage before yours. Were there young people in it?'

He shook his head. *'Nein.* An English lady, by herself.' This time his voice was sympathetic and the indifference in his eyes turned to consternation as I swayed slightly, held up only by my grip on the reins.

I said shakily, 'Before her. In the carriage before her?'

He shook his head again. '*Nein*, Fraulein, the couple who hired it had young children with them, babies. Perhaps if you go yourself to the castle you will find your friends there.' He glanced behind him. 'You will have to wait though. These carriages are all taken, but the ones that have already gone will soon be back.' He smiled reassuringly. 'You will find them — they cannot be far away.'

With renewed horror I saw that the now full carriages were trotting past, and the last two drivers were flicking their reins and beginning to follow them. Another few seconds and I would be stranded and alone. I fought a rising tide of hysteria.

'Please, you must take me with you. *Please*. It's a matter of life and death!'

'The carriage is full, Fraulein.' He was losing patience now and so were his customers. They glared at me, muttering angrily as I tried for the last time. 'The police,' I said frantically. 'The police know all about it. They are on their way here. *Please*, you must take me with you!'

'The carriage is full. It is against the law.' Roughly he tugged the reins from my grasp. 'Now, if you will excuse me.'

Helplessly I stepped back on to the grass verge as the horse brushed past me. The three women and one gentleman, who were the occupants of the carriage, stared down at me curiously, then the man leaned towards me.

'Hippies?' he asked, gesturing to his hair as if it was long.

'Yes, oh yes!'

The woman sitting next to him clicked her tongue reprovingly and pulled at his arm.

'Did they go up to the castle?' I cried.

The carriage was moving away rapidly and I was having to run to keep up with them. He nodded his head vigorously before turning to face his angry wife.

I turned too. I could hear the sound of running footsteps

coming from the direction of the car park, approaching the bend in the road. Once Gunther rounded it, the only people between us would be the small group of women choosing postcards outside the chalet. The last landau clattered past, carrying only three people. I ran after it, calling the driver to stop. He eyed me doubtfully as I thrust a handful of notes into his hand.

'I must . . . go to the castle. Please. It's very important . . .'

He nodded, shoving the notes deep into his pocket before I changed my mind or came to my senses. Gasping for breath I clambered into the carriage, squeezing in beside a large German lady with a pork-pie hat on her head. As I did so I saw the indistinct figure of Gunther between the trees, running towards the bend.

I showered my remaining money to the floor, and amidst the exclamations of alarm and disapproval from the other passengers, dropped on my hands and knees, grovelling between their feet for the scattered coins, struggling to keep my head and body out of sight.

For several minutes I stayed there, bent double, the annoyed women moving their feet out of my way, knocking me with their cumbersome bags. I had to stay out of sight. Out of sight until I had found Annabelle and her friends, or until I could phone Stephen and find out what had happened and what had gone wrong. Dear God, what *could* have gone wrong? My message had been clear enough. Unless . . . I tried to shut the thought from my mind. Unless Gunther had known all along where Stephen was and had silenced him before following me. I shook my head. It wasn't possible, he wouldn't have had the time. From the moment I had seen him outside the newsagent's he had been following me. There had been no opportunity for him to cross the road to the Alte Post. And yet . . . And yet . . . What if Gunther hadn't been by himself? What if Stephen had been murdered while I sat on the coach so foolishly confident. A sob broke from me, and the woman next to me shook my shoulder, and asked if she could help me.

133

I turned my head slightly. The carriage had rounded the next bend of the steepening path. Cautiously I sat back on the seat. The road behind was clear, the chalet out of sight. On either side the dark green trees of the forest pressed in, the only sound that of the horses as they climbed steadily upwards, crushing the thick carpeting of pine needles beneath their hooves.

'*Sind Sie krank*?' the woman asked.

I shook my head.

Not looking too convinced, she rammed her hat even more firmly on her head and settled her bag on her knees. She looked so indomitable, so indefatigable, that for a moment I was tempted to seek her help. But how, in the few words of German I knew, could I explain to her? How could I say, 'Please help me. A fellow countryman of yours is following me and is going to kill me.' And even presuming I could, and she believed me, what could she do?

The two women opposite eyed me warily. Like their companion they were heavily built and sensibly dressed. Both of them were wearing light-weight gaberdines and leather brogues, and on their heads was the same straw-coloured bowler hat with a little feather stuck into the hatband.

I looked away from them, concentrating instead on the winding road below, willing it to stay clear. They had every reason to be disapproving. No doubt they had been spectators to my confrontation with the first driver, and flinging myself to the carriage floor must have confirmed their suspicions that I was best left alone.

Carriages began passing us on their way down to the chalet and fresh customers. I gazed upwards towards the white, limestoned walls of Neuschwanstein, willing the horse to move faster, to hurry towards the last bend and the open gateway of the castle. To the right, the ground fell away in a steep drop to the gorge below. Between the trees I caught a glimpse of the chalet and saw the first of the returning landaus pick up their fares. The fair-haired figure even now beginning his ascent could only be Gunther.

Chapter Sixteen

The next instant, we had rounded the bend and were facing the pinnacles, turrets and battlements of Neuschwanstein. The epitome of every fairy-tale castle I had ever seen, it rose white and shining, glorious against the backdrop of blue lake and snow-capped mountains. The crag of rock on which it was built thrust it high above the surrounding forest, the sea of pine trees merging gradually into the soft green of the plains around Fussen. It was like being on top of the world. Two turrets flanked the gateway building and beneath the gabled entrance hung the Bavarian coat of arms. Through the round arched portal I could see steps leading to an upper courtyard and more towers with narrow, arcaded windows, and slender spires soaring skywards.

A bridge led from the road to the cobbled castle precincts and the driver drew his horse to a halt on reaching it. My three fellow passengers were already fumbling for cameras and getting their guide-books at the ready, but before the horse had turned round on the start of his return journey, I was running over the bridge, through the darkened arch, and into the bright sunlight of the courtyard beyond.

It was thronged with people. Tourists of every shape and size jostled together, forming themselves into groups of thirty or forty around tired-looking guides. Among the babble of voices I could distinguish Italian and French, but there was no sign of Annabelle and her friends and it was fast becoming obvious that, even if they were here, I stood little chance of finding them. I tried to push my way through the mass of camera-slung bodies towards one of the guides. There would be a phone somewhere. I had to find it before Gunther arrived at the bridge. Then I would hide. But the tourists weren't giving way so easily. They stood firm, deliberately preventing me from getting to the front.

A woman shouted at me angrily as I frantically tried to edge round her. Her husband, too, turned.

'I'm not trying to push in.' I tried desperately to make myself clear. 'I just want to know where there is a phone, a *Telefon*.

He shook his head. '*Hier ist kein Telefon.*'

'But there *must* be! Please let me through so that I can ask the guide.'

'*Nein, hier ist kein Telefon.*' They were adamant, turning their backs on me, trapping me so that I could move neither forward nor back. I didn't see Gunther enter the courtyard, all I could see were the heads and shoulders of those surrounding me, but I knew when he had. The familiar icy terror I had felt so often in the last twenty-four hours flooded through me and my hands and face were damp with sweat. The mass of people gave me no feeling of safety, rather the reverse. He would be able to kill me and lose himself among them with no difficulty at all. In fact, if he could ease himself into the crowd I was now in, he could stab me and I wouldn't even fall to the ground! I pressed my hand to my mouth stifling the screams rising within me.

Then we were moving. The crowd began to follow the uniformed guide and I shrank as small as possible, keeping in the centre, hidden, I hoped, by the surrounding bodies. Cold and sick, I shuffled along with them, past the splashing of a fountain and up the steps to the upper courtyard, expecting every moment to feel Gunther's hands upon me.

We drew to a halt again while the guide, first in German, then French, and finally English, informed us that the Palast to the right of us contained the Singers' Hall and two octagonal corner turrets. He enlarged upon the beauty of the frescoes that decorated the inner walls, and pointed out the copper-chased figure of a lion surmounting the gable. The crowd craned their necks and flicked to the appropriate pages in their brochures. I bent my knees, sliding as low as I could, my head bent to the yellow sandstoned ground.

'And there you see the Knights' House.' The heads around me turned in unison to the right. 'This is a two-storied building containing the passages connecting the Square Tower and the Palast with the Knights' House proper rising a storey higher. The intended rich architectural ornamentation was not carried out on account of the early death of the King.' The couple in front murmured sympathetically.

'The German Romanesque style is not only applied to the groined cross-vaults, the framework of the windows and portals, the richly sculptured ornamental work of the passages, but also to the King's rooms, which are divided into two parts by columns and arches. These partitioned rooms . . . ' On and on he went, while those around me listened attentively, referring to their guide-books and easing their weight from one foot to the other. Then, after exhausting his detailed description of the exterior of the Knights' House the guide led the way into the communicating building that connected it with the Square Tower.

I hurried after him, edging as close as I could to the couple in front, not daring to look round in case my eyes should meet Gunther's. Then we were herded up a narrow winding staircase and there was no hope of remaining hidden. If Gunther was on the periphery of the crowd he could not help but see me as I climbed after the others, cruelly exposed in my bright green dress.

I steeled myself to look down, towards the door we had just entered, but there were only suntanned holiday-makers patiently waiting to mount the stairs and endure more of the regimented sight-seeing. I licked my lips nervously. If Gunther was outside or in another part of the castle entirely, there was still a faint chance.

We clustered into a beautiful room with a vaulted ceiling, and a chandelier of gilded brass. The guide paused beneath it, informing us that it contained no less than forty-eight candles. I took his word for it, and tried once more to ease my way to the front. With their attention riveted to the ceiling I managed to squeeze past the couple who had remained so obstinately in front of me, and with many whispered apologies push my way to the edge of the crowd and the guide. I moved towards him as he finished describing the chandelier in French. Seeing my intention he frowned, motioning me to remain where I was as he turned to what he described as the Swan corner.

'Here you can see more of the Lohengrin saga.' He stationed himself in front of the frescoes on the wall, and I struggled manfully to keep my place not too far away from him. 'The swan was the emblem of the Lords of Schwangau and the castle is known as the Castle of the Swan.'

'Excuse me, could . . . '

The guide glared. 'The blue silk drapes and chair coverings are all embroidered with the motif of the swan, as are the iron door-handles.'

He pointed to a flower vase on a tiled stove. 'This vase of Nymphenburg china is also made in the shape of a swan. This favourite animal of King Ludwig appears in every room in the castle. There is no escaping from it.'

No escape. I said defiantly, '*Bitte, wo gibt es ein Telefon?*'

Curtly he turned. 'Madam, I must ask you to remain silent while we are on a tour of inspection of the rooms.'

When I spoke again, my voice was wavering, worn down by the fear, the hopelessness and the heat. 'If you would just tell me where there is a telephone.'

'The nearest telephone is at the restaurant near the car park. And now, ladies and gentlemen, the fresco behind me depicts the miracle of the Holy Grail. According to the legend, the Grail is the Holy chalice Jesus used at the Last Supper and into which Joseph of Arimathea . . . '

The car park. If the nearest phone was at the car park I didn't stand a chance. I clenched my hands into icy knots, shaking my head, trying to clear it of the words 'no escape, no escape', trying to think positively.

'This chalice was preserved in the Castle Monsalvat, specially built for it and watched by the knighthood that served the Grail and fought for right and justice. When . . . '

He couldn't be talking in English to only me! I said suddenly, 'Would you ask who else is English here, please?'

'Madam!' he hissed. I ignored him and turned, desperate with hope. 'Is anyone here English, please?'

Curious and displeased faces stared back at me as I waited in vain. The guide spoke to me through clenched teeth. 'Madam, for the last time . . . '

'I'm sorry, but . . . '

'When Elsa of Brabant is innocently accused, God grants her prayers by sending Lohengrin, the Knight of the Grail, to fight for her. Therefore, the name 'Lohengrin' is to be seen on the chalice. On the wall . . . ' he continued firmly, studiously avoiding looking in my direction. 'On the wall where the entrance is, Lohengrin's arrival in Antwerp. In the recess . . . '

I stared unseeingly. There must be some way of escape. My powers of reasoning seemed to be frozen. The castle wasn't so big, sooner or later Gunther was going to catch up with this particular party of tourists. What was the most sensible thing to do?

My first idea, that of seeking help from the guides, seemed less practicable now I was face to face with one of them. Presuming they had a rest-room and let me stay in it, Gunther would simply do what he had done at Nordlingen: explain that I was mentally disturbed and that he was my doctor. After my bizarre story the guides would need very little persuasion. Courteously he would thank them, apologize for any trouble I had caused . . . and lead me away. To kill me with as little effort as it takes to swat a fly. The guide's persistent voice broke in on my thoughts.

'He defeats Telramund thus proving Elsa's innocence. Lohengrin becomes Elsa's husband on condition that she should never enquire from where he comes . . . '

Any chance of leaving the castle and travelling back to the car park was utterly remote. If there had been a delay in Stephen being given my message (I refused to contemplate the fact that Gunther might have had Ellis or Levos with him in Oberammergau and that Stephen might be dead). If he hadn't

139

received the message straight away he surely would have by now. Any minute and the castle would be swarming with police. All I had to do was hide from Gunther until they arrived. The guide may have been right in that there was no escape from the castle, but in the castle . . . '

'After some time, Elsa, in spite of having promised, asks the question, thus destroying her happiness. Lohengrin has to leave Elsa and his two little sons.'

In a castle like this, there must be one corner or recess in which a young woman weighing only eight stone could hide.

The people around me began to move once more.

'The next room is the King's dressing-room. Here the impression was intended of an open bower with the blue sky above.'

I let them file past me, scouring the room for any place that could offer a hidey-hole. There were no cupboards, only panelled walls of oak and the richly covered stools and chairs covered with blue silk. The long curtains that fell behind each white stuccoed pillar were caught half-way down and gathered back, offering no hope of concealment. I could hear more people climbing the staircase leading to the room and I hurried after my own party, worming my way into their centre again. By this time I was conscious that I was regarded very much as an eccentric, as they made room for me, grumbling and holding their cameras and handbags well out of my reach.

The guide was saying in his monotonous voice, 'The ceiling is painted sky-blue with clouds and birds, around the sides a trellis with clinging vine, the painting on the wall is of the Meistersinger Hans Sachs and of the minstrel Walther von Stolzing. The birds teach Walther how to sing . . . '

There wasn't room to hide a thimble. The only furnishings were a richly carved washstand with a pretty toilet-set, and a small table with a jewel-box. As I listened to the guide extolling the beauties of the metal work on the doors I tried to decide which was safest. To stay with the group until I could see somewhere I might hide, or leave them and hurry through the castle by myself, searching for a place? If I came face to face with Gunther on my own . . .

'And now the Oratory. This small chapel is devoted to St Louis, the patron saint of King Ludwig. On the altar, in the centre of the triptych, St Louis. The crucifix is of ivory.'

There was not enough room to walk into it, and those around me peered forwards to catch a glimpse of the altar and the praying desk covered in violet velvet and lavish gold embroidery. Since we had climbed the stairs I had been unable to see down into the courtyard or on to the steep path leading up through the woods. Surely the police would be on their way by now? I looked at my watch. It was twelve-fifteen. Where in the world were they?

'And now this next room was the King's private dining-room. It is a comparatively small room as the King used to dine alone and there were never any feasts. The dishes were brought up from the kitchen by means of a food-lift in the corridor. In contrast to the other castles there is no magic table which may be lowered into the floor. On the walls . . . '

Opposite me, set in the centre of the wall, was a large door with ornate metal hinges. Red silk curtains hung at either side of it from a polished wooden rail, and in front of it, barring the way, was a Romanesque chair. Wherever it led, it was obviously not in the official itinerary.

'The pictures on the walls are all from the times of the minstrels. The centre-piece of the table is a sculpture in gilded bronze showing Siegfried fighting the dragon. The base of the table decoration is polished marble and weighs two hundred and fifty pounds.'

By sheer will-power I prevented myself from running over there and then to see if the door opened. I forced myself to stand still, to wait until he had described in painful detail the wall painting and the unusual ceiling, the ferns and thistles surrounding Siegfried and the dragon. Then, as they moved forward once more, I hung back, hoping against hope. The last straggler left the room and I ran over to the door. The handle was hidden by the chair and I had to move the chair forward, off the wood floor on which it stood on to the carpeting.

141

It was very heavy and I could hear the next party enter the Oratory. It would only take a few minutes to describe the few furnishings in there. Panting, I pulled the chair clear of the door, grasping the heavy metal handle. My fingers slipped, sticky with sweat, as I strained at the stiff bolt. The guide was describing the altar.

Frantically I pushed for all I was worth, but it didn't move. Now he was describing the praying desk. I tugged and strained, panic rising in my throat until I thought I would choke. Then the handle turned, opening into what must have been a servants' room but was now bare and empty and obviously not open to public view. I heaved the chair back off the carpet, pulling the door to, and edging the chair back into its original position as near as I was able. It was impossible to pull it as far back as it had been, but I managed to get it clear of the carpet, and at least straight, before I closed the door and sank shivering and trembling to the floor.

Chapter Seventeen

I just sat there, head against the wall, legs stretched out in front of me, eyes closed. Dimly I was aware of the sound of people entering the room beyond, and of the guide lecturing monotonously on the paintings and the wooden ceiling. His voice broke over me in waves of German, French, English, then it receded, as he led the way into the next room, followed by the shuffling feet of the tourists. I breathed a sigh of relief. If he hadn't noticed anything wrong with the chair's position then the chances were that successive guides wouldn't either.

I opened my eyes. There was a window set in the wall opposite, but it was too high to see out of and there were no chairs or anything else on which to stand. The room was completely bare. I closed my eyes again, incapable of feeling any further frustration or anxiety.

I was tired. Dog tired. Tired of everything. The continual flight, the fear, the doubt. It had been two days since I had slept. Really slept. Faint sounds from the courtyard below drifted up and into the room. If there was a great hue and cry I would be bound to hear it. Until then, I would sleep.

Intermittently I half-woke, stiff and uncomfortable on the hard floor, but only long enough to settle my head on to my shoulder-bag, find a fresh position and doze off again. When I did finally wake it was because of the cold. I sat up, rubbing my arms and shivering. The sunlight that had streamed through the window had been replaced by quickly falling twilight. I stared at my watch unbelievingly. It was half-past eight. I jumped to my feet. *Half-past eight*! Stephen would be out of his mind with worry. And where was everyone?

I stood motionless in the centre of the room. There wasn't

143

a sound. Hurriedly I searched through my bag for my literature. In the fast dwindling light I read: The castle is open to the public, May 1st to Oct 31st. 8.30 am to 5.30 pm.

Five-thirty! Dear God, I'd already been locked in for three hours! Hastily I opened the door, pushing it against the heavy chair outside until there was room for me to squeeze out. Then I halted. The room was lit only by moonlight and looked enormous and mysterious.

It seemed, as I stood in the near darkness, surrounded by the grossness of King Ludwig's fantasy, that all the fear I had felt in the past had been nothing but a prelude. Nothing but a foretaste of what was happening to me now. Through open doors, other rooms led off, the walls lined with scenes of knights and minstrels, saints and kings, the interiors cluttered with pillars and columns, the high vaulted ceiling echoing every sound. Through the day it had been the fairy-tale castle of Cinderella, the sanctuary of a romantic maniac. Now, in the shadows of approaching night, the medieval splendour was grotesque, the suits of armour and sumptuous hangings, macabre. The thought of spending the night alone, locked in this edifice to a dead legend, was horrifying.

The barren rooms were alive with the spirits of the figures thronging the walls. The silence, the isolation of the castle perched high on the mountain-top, was overwhelming. In these Bavarian forests tales of vampires and werewolfs were still prevalent and my twentieth-century common sense vanished as I stared with dread into the deepening gloom.

I dug my nails into my palms, forcing myself to move. If I didn't go now while there was still some light to see by, I would never find my way out. Apprehensively I skirted the table in the centre of the room, crossing the ante-room at the far side and going out into the passage, my footsteps echoing and re-echoing on the bare floor.

Stifling all thoughts of the supernatural, I hurried past the dragon's head lanterns on the wall, averting my eyes from the scenes of hunting and killing beneath them, intent only on reaching the top of the stairs. The faint light that glimmered through a stained glass window was barely sufficient for me to see my way down them, and I had to hug the wall, feeling my way into utter blackness. Carefully I edged down step by step, my hands running feverishly along the smooth wood, feeling my way to the heavy, oak door at the bottom.

By the time I reached it I was in a cold sweat, expecting any minute to hear the clanking of ghostly chains. Blindly I felt over the door for the handle and pulled hard. Nothing happened. Again and again I twisted and turned it, pulling with all my might, but it was no use. The door was locked. I didn't know whether it was beads of perspiration or tears that were dripping down my face. I only knew that when they opened the door in the morning they would find a raging maniac beating and clawing at the wood. I pressed my hands against my cheeks, struggling for self-control. I must force myself to go back up the stairs and find another way out. Trembling, I turned, groping my way upwards, my mouth dry and parched.

Moonlight shone through the arched window on the landing, lighting my way as I hesitated between the King's apartments on my right and a marbled doorway on my left. The darkness seemed less intense on the left hand side, and with my heart beating painfully against my chest, I stepped beneath the arch.

My feet clicked on to mosaic tiles and pale, silvery light streamed through two tiers of windows, illuminating a huge cavern of a place, glittering and gleaming with gold and silver, ivory and lapis lazuli. A flight of marble stairs led up to an apse of Byzantine splendour, with Christ, his apostles and angels, soaring in glory beneath a golden dome. Tremulously I walked to the foot of the stairs, but the semi-circle at the top, guarded by giant brass candelabra, led nowhere. I turned, lifting my eyes to the second tier of windows where a narrow gallery encircled three sides of the room. There had to be a way leading up to it. Bars of moonlight shone down on to the centre of the floor, leaving the far recesses impenetrable.

I clicked my way across to the polished columns of

porphyric rock, then slipped, my heart in my mouth, into the blackness beyond. Edging forward inch by inch my foot stumbled on the first step, then the second. Minutes later I stood at the high windows looking down on to the spectacular view of forest and gorge, with the mountains beyond, stark and white beneath the star-filled sky. Far below was the shiny surface of the lake and the dark outline of Hohenschwangau. As I watched I saw the pin-prick of car lights approaching the lake, disappearing into the thick woods, then reappearing again, this time nearer.

I stiffened, straining to see in the darkness. Seconds later they flickered again at the foot of the gorge. 'Dear God,' I whispered. 'Let it be Stephen. It *must* be Stephen!'

With renewed hope I stumbled back down the stairs, my footsteps ringing metallically on the tesselated floor as I hurriedly crossed it back into the corridor. There was no other way down into the courtyard from here, but perhaps if I climbed the staircase to the next floor I would have better luck.

I trod warily, my hands sliding along the smooth wood of the walls as the stairs climbed higher and higher. Gradually, slender shafts of moonlight pierced the inky blackness and I breasted the landing, gazing unbelievingly at what appeared to be a huge palm tree of marble rising from the centre of the stairs, merging into the ceiling above me.

I paused, trying to get my bearings. I had turned to my left on the lower landing, therefore if there was another staircase leading down to the courtyard it must be on the right. Carefully I stepped past a stone dragon, heading in what I hoped was the right direction, peering once more into the shadows.

The room was even more splendid than the last. A polished wood floor stretched endlessly down to what could have been a stage, more giant candelabras, visible only as dimly looming shapes, flanked the walls, and hanging in the half-light above my head were golden, crown-shaped chandeliers.

Purposefully I began to walk to the lower end of the room,

scanning the walls, searching for a doorway. As I did so I became aware of another sound other than my own footsteps. Somebody was moving through the room below me.

I stood perfectly still. I had been so obsessed with the need to escape from the castle that I had forgotten Gunther and the possibility that he, too, had hidden away . . . And now he was here, bringing death closer and closer.

I tip-toed to the wall and pressed myself flat against it. The darkness here was thick and black. Below me was the stealthy tread of feet. I hugged the wall, this time completely without hope, stupefied, motionless with fear.

Then I heard him flick a match. There was a soft step; another. From outside came the screech of an owl swooping on its prey; the heavy rustle of the wind in the trees, and then silence.

If he should mount the stairs . . .

With slow deliberation the footsteps changed course, hesitated for a fraction of a second, and then began to climb. I couldn't breathe. I couldn't swallow. I was rooted to the spot. My heart felt as if it was bursting within me as I stared, rigid with terror, into the darkness.

Then it was still, the only sound that of the owl, hooting as it flew past the windows. I licked my lips. I had to move, to act: he couldn't find me here, cowering against the wall. *I had to move* . . .

There was the warm trickle of blood beneath my nails where they had dug into my palms. My body was trembling, shaking from head to toe. I pressed my hands against the wall behind me and began carefully, oh so carefully, to inch my way along it.

He was still there. Listening and waiting. The slightest sound and he would be upon me. I could see the stage now, half-formed and insubstantial in the darkness, and above it, a gallery.

I strained my eyes, trying to discern what was real and what was shadow, the blood pounding in my temples. My heel knocked the edge of a chair. I froze, sick with panic, but no

147

other sound broke the silence. Stealthily I slipped one foot out of my shoe, then the other. If I could reach the gallery I wouldn't be as easy to find. He would pass me by, search somewhere else . . .

He began to climb once more - unhurried, purposeful, as if he knew just where to find me. I could hear the sound of his hand sliding over the banister and the sharp click of a ring or watch as it came into contact with the stone dragon at the top of the stairs. In a state of semi-consciousness I reached the narrow steps to the gallery, my stockinged feet slippery on the polished wood as I flew upwards.

Behind me were the windows looking down on to the gorge and forest. I bent double, huddling beneath them, straining to hear his next move. Although I couldn't see him, I knew he was standing at the entrance to the room. The blood pounded in my temples so loudly I thought it must give me away, but he didn't move. The wind rushed through the tops of the trees far below and over and above it came the sound of his shallow breathing.

Hardly able to suppress the sobs that choked my throat I stared round with aching eyes, praying for a miracle. The cool lick of the wind touched my cheek. I craned my neck, searching for its source. It came again, this time quite unmistakably. Somewhere, not very far away from me, there was access to fresh air and freedom.

Stealthily I edged forward, every inch an agony of suspense. Through the thick darkness I could sense him listening, the slightest sound . . .

My heart was beating light and fast as I saw from where the breeze was coming. It looked like a door, but to reach it I still had two windows to pass. Windows which would silhouette me clearly against the star-filled sky.

With every nerve in my body screaming at me to break loose, to run, I crouched down slowly, very slowly, every minute stretching into years. Carefully I dropped to my hands and knees, placed one hand in front of the other, and began to move forward.

From outside the wind raced through the tops of the trees, the cold draught luring me on like a lifeline. Imperceptibly I drew nearer, then, just as I was about to straighten up again, he moved. The soft tread of crepe-soled shoes stepped hesitatingly forwards. I froze, holding my breath. He was moving down the centre of the room, away from me but in the direction of the steps that led to the gallery. The sweet night air blew full in my face as I rose, fraction by fraction, towards its source.

Then I stopped, the breath driven out of my body. It wasn't a door. It was only a window that had been left ajar. Another second and I think I would have broken. I couldn't take any more. It would be easier to be caught, to get it over with rather than prolong the nightmare.

I was vaguely aware that he, too, had stopped. Outside, the stars were now veiled with cloud and I could see the dark gleam of the water far, far below. I leaned forward, touching the cold pane of the glass lightly with my finger. Then I stiffened, staring with aching eyes into the night beyond. A foot or two beneath the window was a narrow parapet of stone running the length of the wall. But even as the idea half-formed, it vanished. To step out there would be suicide. There was nothing but a sheer drop to the black depths of the gorge, hundreds of feet below.

He laughed softly to himself, the sound carrying and magnifying beneath the vaulted ceiling. I could hear him pick up my sandals, tapping the heels lightly together.

'They're still warm, Cinderella. This time your ball has come well and truly to an end.'

His voice was gay, caressing almost. 'Your Mr Maitland is dead, Susan. Would you like me to tell you how your knight on a white charger over-reached himself?' He laughed again. 'By the time I've finished with you, Fraulein Carter, you'll be glad to join him. Very glad.'

He began to walk easily towards the stage, all stealth abandoned.

I had no choice. I swung the window open and lowered

149

myself on to the windswept ledge.

I backed against the rough stone. It was icy cold, and my nails, scratching desperately for a handhold, could find nothing on which to grip. The wind smacked into me, pinioning me against the wall. Without it, I don't think I would have survived more than a second. The ledge was no more than two feet wide and I pressed my head and shoulders back and up, facing the vast dome of the sky.

Somehow I had to make myself look down. I had to see how far the ledge extended along the castle face; I braced myself and, with a soundless prayer, tentatively turned my head. The world swung crazily, sky and gorge whirling together in a hideous kaleidoscope that sucked at me, sweeping me giddily into its vortex.

I shut my eyes tight, eardrums bursting, fighting for survival. Gunther's voice sliced into my nightmare, cruel and harsh.

'You God-damned, stupid bitch!' My shoes were hurled violently against a far wall. His words whipped past me on the wind, carrying out into the black void that surrounded me, sailing out over ridge after ridge of mountains, falling, falling . . . like a leaf spiralling down . . . down . . .

'No!' I shouted. 'No, no, no!'

He laughed then, only inches away from me.

If he stretched out, tugged at my skirt . . .

I began to move, my palms outstretched behind me. Raising one foot, I pressed myself back, fractionally shifting my weight, drawing my other foot to meet it, dragging my head along the crumbling stone until I was once more carefully balanced a bare six inches further along the ledge. Again I drew the other to meet it . . .

'What the . . . !' He leaned as far out of the window as possible, lunging at me, but I was beyond his grasp. His hands smacked futilely on the naked walls.

I laughed then, half insane with fear. I heard his breath hiss and for a second thought I had defeated him. But I hadn't. He simply moved back against the window embrasure, carefully positioning himself, his right arm extended towards me at eye level. Another minute and I would be blasted to kingdom come.

Lost in my own private hell. I still kept shifting along the narrow ledge. So he had a gun. Of course he had a gun. The wind tugged at my skirt, beating it against the stone. From a distant turret the owl hooted and still I kept on edging inch by inch, waiting for him to pull the trigger, submerged in a sea of unreality. How could I have thought that by stepping out thousands of feet above the valley I could escape him? Hadn't the guide said that there was no escape . . . none . . .

'You've cheated me, Susan,' he said, the old mockery back. 'I had such plans for you. Still, all the best medieval maidens died virgins. Plunging into an abyss to propitiate the Gods was quite the done thing. All in all, I find it quite apt.'

Through half-open eyes I could just make out the corner of the wall. The moon had sailed behind cloud now and I could see nothing of the sheer drop beneath me. I was isolated in an impenetrable void. I kept on moving, inch by excrutiating inch. Perhaps it was too dark for Gunther to see where the castle ended and thin air began. Perhaps if I rounded the corner before he tired of my terror . . .

'A killing in a lonely field or ditch would have been wasted on you, Susan. This is much more your style.'

The owl swooped out of the vast emptiness, curving down into the depths below.

'It's a great pity I don't have the time or opportunity to drown you in the Starnbergersee as Ludwig died. That would have been even more theatrical.'

The corner was a mere yard away. *If* I took bigger steps . . .

'And if you think you are going to reach that corner, you are an even bigger fool than I thought.' The mockery had gone, the game was drawing to a close.

I could hear him fumbling with his left hand for his cigarette-case, was vaguely aware of the tiny spurt of flame as he lit it, could almost see the sensual pleasure on his lips as he leaned back, inhaling deeply, toying with me like a spider a

151

fly.

'Even you must have wondered at the interest I was taking in you. Do you really think you are so desirable that I would run round after you, behaving like an English vicar or boy scout, grateful for any crumbs that came my way?' He laughed derisively. 'Take it from me, Miss Prim and Proper Carter, you're not worthy of a second glance.'

There was a roaring in my ears as I tried to shut his voice out of my consciousness. The world was beginning to spiral again, and I knew I was going to be violently sick.

'And you had the affontery to turn me down . . . ' His voice was savage. 'Well, you're going to pay for it, Fraulein Carter. You're going to pay.'

I stood motionless on my narrow ledge, watching the moon slide from behind a bank of cloud, tipping the peaks of the snow-covered Alps, the tears streaming down my face, the wind whipping my hair across my eyes.

Please don't let it last any longer, I remember thinking. And then: Stephen . . . *Stephen*! . . .

'Here it comes, you bitch. Here it comes.'

There was a sharp crack. My legs jerked convulsively under me, and with the sound of my own screams ringing in my ears, I plunged downwards.

Chapter Eighteen

The world swam dizzily, split with noise and lights. There was the thud of feet running down the gallery and strange hands seized hold of me. The blood was throbbing in my ears. The chandeliers, the ceiling, were spinning crazily. From a far distance came voices, breathless and relieved, then another shout . . . this time peremptory and sharp. I was being lifted into a sitting position and someone thrust my head roughly between my knees.

I cried out, and the thundering in my ears eased, the giddiness subsided. I raised my head, squinting dazedly against the bright light that shone in my face. A young man was holding me, speaking to me in a voice I did not recognize, then more people burst into the room below. There was the sharp crack of a pistol, then another; I struggled unsteadily, trying to free myself of the restraining hands, my terror flooding back.

The firm grip increased. The torchlight that had been shining full in my face was directed down to the far end of the gallery, lighting the way for the booted feet that drummed past us. The noise, the shouts increased.

'What *is* it? What's *happening*?' I yelled, wrenching myself away, forcing my shaking legs to take my weight.

Hands closed about me once more. There was the sound of shattering glass, a long, dreadful scream, then silence.

I knew then; as time stood still, the running feet were suddenly silent, the only sound that of the wind rushing through the tops of the distant trees outside.

'Stephen!' I cried, vainly trying to free myself. 'Stephen!'

The man beside me gave a brusque exclamation, his grip tightening. The shapes in the darkness broke up, lights criss-crossed the ceiling, sweeping the frescoed walls and polished floor. A police officer strode towards us, sheathing his gun, but I was hardly aware of him.

'*Sind Sie verletzt?*' he asked the man who supported me. Then, in a gentler voice: 'Everything is all right, Fraulein. We'll have you safely back in Oberammergau in half an hour.'

I stared past him to the blood-stained figure slowly following him.

'Stephen! Oh, sweet heaven, *Stephen*!' The policeman let me go and Stephen caught me with one arm, laughing unsteadily.

'Easy does it, darling. It's all right now. It's all right.'

'They've shot you . . . your arm . . . '

His left arm hung limp, the blood flowing freely down it, staining my dress a rich scarlet.

'It's nothing, darling. Only a graze. Truly.'

I began to cry. 'I . . . I . . . thought you were dead. I heard that scream . . . and . . . '

His hand gripped my hair tightly. 'It was Gunther, Susan. He fell.'

I stared at his cut face and bleeding mouth.

'Stephen, what . . . '

'It was an accident, Susan. We were fighting and he lost his balance.'

'But he had a gun!'

He squeezed my shoulder. 'Yes, I know, darling.'

'But how . . . '

'Later, Susan. First things first.'

Surrounded by armed police and the beam of powerful torches raking the gorge for Gunther's broken body, he kissed me. A long, long time later he let me go, and the words he whispered to me then were for me alone and not for repeating.

The police officer cleared his throat. 'Your arm, Herr Maitland. *Bitte*.' He bound it tightly above the elbow, grinning down at me. 'I told the Fraulein everything was well, yes?'

'Yes,' I said faintly.

'If the Fraulein could hurry,' he said, turning to Stephen again. 'There are still a lot of questions to be answered.'

154

'Can't that wait until morning?' asked Stephen, his good arm firmly round me as we made our way across the echoing floor and out into the corridor.

'Yes. Fraulein Carter has suffered only shock. The doctor will give a sedative and tomorrow we will come to the hotel.'

Stephen said, 'You hear that, Pearl White? You've only suffered shock.'

'Shock,' I said grimly, fumbling for the hand-rail on the outer wall of the staircase, 'is quite enough.'

With his assistance I managed to climb down the stairs and walk unsteadily into the cold night air. Through the gateway were two cars, and there was the sound of more speeding up the mountain road. They rounded the last bend, grinding to a spectacular halt, headlights blazing. But before any more police could spill out into the starlit courtyard, instructions were shouted at them and they began to reverse. The night was ripped by the roar of their engines as they sped back the way they had come.

'It shouldn't take long,' the officer remarked, opening the door of the car for me.

'Long for what?' I asked, slipping across the smooth leather of the seat, Stephen's body close beside me.

'To pick up the pieces.'

I concentrated hard on not being sick.

'I . . . I suppose there's no chance he's still alive, is there?' I said, turning to Stephen.

'From that height even if he'd landed at the foot of the walls he would have been dashed to pieces. As it is − ' he shrugged − 'he must have dropped straight into the gorge. The woods are so thick it may take them a little time to find him . . . '

I leaned back against his shoulder, taking a shuddering breath, grateful for the cool breeze that blew in through the open window and for his arm, loving and protective, around me.

As we dipped down through the pines I had a last glimpse of Neuschwanstein, towering black and jagged against the night sky, then the headlights sliced a brilliant path through the rapidly enclosing forest, and it was gone.

'Who shot you?'

Stephen grinned. 'The local constabulary. But they didn't have much choice.'

'What happened up there? Was it you who pulled me inside?'

'Of course, my love. There was a cool breeze. Another minute and you would have caught your death.'

'Too true,' I said feelingly. 'But it wouldn't have been with cold. How come you arrived before the police?'

'I didn't. The officer at Oberammergau –' Stephen nodded in the direction of the man in the front seat – 'and three of his men and myself came together, for reasons which I will explain later,' he added hurriedly as I opened my mouth to ask another question. 'I was under strict instructions to behave myself and not get in the way. They began a swift search of the King's apartments, and I, not being very good at discipline, went up to the Singers' Hall.'

'Is that what it was?'

'You mean you didn't even notice the frescoes?'

'Not one.'

'Well, Gunther was too engrossed in your little tête-à-tête to hear me creeping about. I came into the room seconds after you'd stepped on to the parapet, but unfortunately the police had already relieved me of my borrowed pistol. If they hadn't I'd have shot him there and then. If I had gone back for the police and they had burst into the room, he would have shot you immediately, and if he hadn't, the sound of the police firing at him would have sent you over the edge. I managed to climb up the stairs to the gallery and crawled along to the window on the far side of you. Gunther was about ten yards away, but he was propped in the window and intent on you. If I'd reached out for you then, he would have shot us both, so I just prayed he'd keep talking long enough for the police to arrive and for me to grab you when they did. It wasn't much fun,' he said, his voice reflecting a little of what he had

156

suffered. 'Then it seemed as if time had run out and he was finally going to shoot, so I grabbed your legs and pulled you backwards.'

'And the police burst into the room?'

'Thank God,' said Stephen devoutly.

'So the shots I heard were the police firing at Gunther?'

'Yes. He would have made an easy target up there against the window and would have been wasting his time trying to shoot into the dark below, so he bolted. I'd thrown myself on top of you, but he just leaped over us and ran down the gallery, presumably to find a better vantage point to shoot from. And I went after him.'

'But why? The police had arrived, we were safe.'

'What sort of a man do you think I am?' he asked quietly. 'That bastard abuses, manhandles and tries to murder you, and you think I should just have stayed where it was safe and let the police deal with him! I'd have knocked hell out of him for what he did to you at the farm alone.'

'Did you . . . kill him?' I asked hesitantly.

He was silent for a minute, then he said slowly, 'Not intentionally. I brought him down with a tackle and we were fighting for the gun. I managed to prize it from his hand and he was trying to force me back against the window. By this time the police were racing down the gallery towards us and two shots were fired, one of them catching me in the arm. Gunther seemed quite oblivious of them, he was so intent on forcing me through that window. He damn near succeeded too. I twisted to one side as he hit out, and his own momentum hurled him to his death.'

'I see,' I said, clasping his hand tightly in the dark. 'What I *don't* see is why it took you so long to arrive. What happened?'

He shook his head in mock reproach. 'You may well ask. There was only one small thing wrong with the hare-brained plan you concocted on realizing Gunther was following you. And that was your note.'

'I don't understand. I told you where I was going, didn't I?'

157

'Oh, you did that all right,' he agreed affably. 'But you wrote the name of the wrong hotel on the note.'

'I did not!' I exclaimed, sitting bolt upright. 'I wrote, Stephen Maitland, Hotel Furstenhaus.'

'The Furstenhaus,' said Stephen patiently, 'is the hotel Gunther booked you into, hoping to lead me there. The Alte Post is the hotel I'm staying at.'

I could only stare at him, appalled.

'The manager of the Furstenhaus accepted the note when Mrs Bosemann said it was from Miss Susan Carter. After all, he still had you booked down to arrive.'

'Oh Stephen,' I said, mortified, 'how could I have been so *dim*.'

'I've no idea, darling. But as I love you I'll overlook it this time. Just don't make a habit of it.'

And he kissed me, long and hard, driving away every vestige of nightmare. After a little while I said, 'What did you do when I didn't return?'

'*That*,' he said emphatically, 'I prefer to forget. We owe a lot to the indefatigable Mrs Bosemann. The manager's reluctant acceptance of your note had caused her some apprehension and she went back there at seven to see you and check that things had worked out between us both. The manager finally explained that he had no Mr Maitland in his hotel, and that, as yet, Fraulein Carter hadn't arrived herself. She demanded the note back and Mr Bosemann mentioned that you had said the hotel *just across the road*. Well, the Furstenhaus is quite a way from where you handed over the note, so they retraced their steps. At the third try they asked for me at the Alte Post. The officer and three of his men were with me then, and the receptionist put it on one side, not wanting to bother me!'

'I don't believe it!'

He laughed. 'Half the police force in the country had been looking for you all the afternoon, *and* interrogating me. I think they thought I was a professional hoaxer wasting police time. They didn't believe a word I told them about Cliburn or that your life was in danger. Isn't that right, Officer?'

The officer laughed. 'We *did* begin a search, Mr Maitland.'

'Maybe. But it wasn't until the receptionist absentmindedly said a note had been handed in for me and they read it that I was finally believed. Though once they knew it was for real, they certainly moved. I insisted on coming with them and they didn't waste time arguing. Within seconds we were on the road to Neuschwanstein with orders out to every policeman in the district to follow.'

'And Mrs Bosemann?'

Stephen clapped his hand to his forehead. 'Good Lord, I'd forgotten all about her. She'll be wondering what on earth is going on.'

'Never mind,' I said. 'She'll have Mr Bosemann to comfort her, and we'll make it up to her when we get back.'

'And to each other,' said Stephen, and kissed me again.

Minutes later the car swept into the open clearing beside the lake. It was alive with the shadowy figures of policemen and the dark shapes of their cars and of an ambulance. Strong beams of light scanned the forest and there came the sound of many feet beating a way through the bushes and low-hanging branches, searching. I turned my head away quickly.

'All right, my love?' Stephen asked tenderly.

'Yes. All I need is a decent meal and a good night's sleep.'

'That's my girl.'

With my head cradled on his shoulder I closed my eyes, and long before we reached Oberammergau I was fast asleep.

Chapter Nineteen

I hardly remember going to bed that night. The strain of the past twenty-four hours had well and truly caught up with me and I allowed myself to be escorted meekly into the hotel and to my room. I was vaguely aware of the activity around me, of the doctor coming and giving me a sedative, and of the many policemen who seemed to fill the hotel's tiny foyer. And I remember Stephen's kiss before he went off with the doctor to have his arm attended to. Then I clambered slowly into bed, sliding down between the clean, crisp sheets, asleep as soon as my head touched the pillow.

I woke to a soft knocking on my door and the sound of the birds singing in the beech tree outside my room. For a few minutes I was filled with a nameless dread, then a great wave of relief swept over me as memory returned. The sun was shining gloriously outside and Stephen had said he loved me. The knock came again, louder this time.

'Come in,' I called, pushing myself up against the pillows.

Stephen stepped into the room, a tray with coffee and croissants precariously balanced in one hand.

'This is your very own room service. No one else gets breakfast in bed at twelve o'clock on a Saturday morning.'

'Twelve!' I stared at him unbelievingly.

'Twelve,' he repeated blandly. 'And there's half the German C.I.D waiting to speak to you downstairs. And a roomful of reporters and photographers and . . . '

'You're joking,' I said horrified, and now wide awake.

'About the police, no. The reporters and photographers, yes. But give them another couple of hours and they'll be here.'

'Then I most decidedly won't be,' I said, eating a roll hungrily. 'Stephen, I'm absolutely starving. I haven't had a proper meal since . . . well, it's so long ago I can't bear to think of it. I can't survive on a couple of rolls.'

'These are just to give you enough strength to get dressed and come downstairs. Your lunch is on the table. You *were* offered a meal last night before you went to bed, but I doubt if you could have stayed awake long enough to have eaten it. Feel better now?'

'Lots. And you? Is your arm okay?'

'Yes, I wasn't being the brave hero when I said it was only grazed. Though it did bleed rather spectacularly, didn't it? Anyway, you hurry up and come downstairs. Our friend from last night is panting to question you.'

'I've got quite a few questions to ask myself.'

Stephen sat down on the edge of the bed. 'They found him just before daylight, Susan.'

I put down my cup of coffee slowly.

'His real name was Carl Mugler. His father was Heinrich Mugler, the Nazi war criminal.'

'Oh,' I said, in a flat voice.

Stephen took the cup and held my hand in his.

'After the war, Mugler and his wife and son escaped to Brazil. The wife died soon afterwards, but Heinrich Mugler lived very prosperously, changing his identity and background completely. Carl was sent to an expensive English school and there was nothing to connect them with the past. Until the late nineteen sixties, that is. Herr Ahlers had worked unceasingly to bring to justice the criminals of the war. He himself was a Jew. For thirty years they had no more information of Heinrich Mugler than that he was missing, presumed dead. Until Georg Kern was arrested in Uraguay. And what Kern said led Ahlers to believe that Mugler was still alive. The hunt intensified and Heinrich Mugler was caught and sentenced for his war crimes two years ago.'

'I remember it. He was at Auschwitz.'

'Yes. Well, his son wanted revenge. He hired Ellis and Levos to do the killing while he stayed down here under an assumed name. Even if his cover had been blown he would have had

161

witnesses to prove he was nowhere near Bonn when Ahlers was shot. He very nearly got away with it too. Ellis and Levos left the city in the stolen car, which wasn't reported missing until hours after they had gone. And at the moment in time when they crashed, the police had no lead on them whatsoever. Gunther would have paid them at the farmhouse and then the three of them would have split and they might never have been caught. As it is, Ellis was arrested in London a couple of hours ago and it's only a matter of time before they bring in Levos.'

'I think he was mad,' I said, staring at the sunlit branches of the beech tree. 'To behave like he did . . . '

'Susan.' Stephen tilted my chin so that I was looking straight at him. 'It's no use brooding about it. It happened, and now it's over. And another thing I want to say . . . '

'Yes?'

'I love you.'

Later, when he had gone downstairs and I had washed and dressed, I knew he was right. Already, the events of the last forty-eight hours were dimming. I felt on top of the world and more than capable of answering any questions the police might ask. As it happened, they didn't ask many. Stephen had spent all the morning with them and all they wanted from me was confirmation.

The inspector's formal departure was spoiled somewhat by Mrs Bosemann rushing up the pathway, arms outstretched.

'Honey, are you okay?'

The policemen hurriedly stepped out of her way as she split their ranks, rushing straight through them towards the veranda.

'We've been so *worried*, honey.' She clasped me to her bosom. 'Is everything okay now? My, you don't look a bit well. What you need is a good square meal.'

'I've just had one,' I protested, laughing. 'And yes, Mrs Bosemann, everything's okay now.'

'Well, thank heavens. What a time we've had! First we handed your note over like you asked and the young man was most reluctant to take it. Hamilton and I couldn't understand it. I wasn't at all easy in my mind, not at all. I said to Hamilton, "There's something wrong." Didn't I, honey?'

Mr Bosemann stood beaming behind his excited wife, nodding assent.

'So we went back there to see you, to make sure everything was all right, and when the man said you weren't even booked in there yet and he had no one by the name of Maitland, well! Honey, we didn't know what to do. I demanded the note back of course, and then Hamilton remembered that you had said the hotel just across the road. We searched and searched, but there wasn't another hotel by that name so we just went into them all, asking for Mr Maitland, and when we *did* find it, the receptionist said she would see Mr Maitland got the message but that he couldn't be disturbed at the moment. Well, that didn't please me, I can tell you. Hamilton and I decided to wait in the garden. We ordered a couple of drinks, and sat at the table over there, beneath the trees and then . . . what a commotion! Policemen everywhere, rushing off as though there was a fire, and no one able to tell us what was happening! Honey, I can't begin to describe the night we've spent. I've been out of my mind with worry.'

I gently disentangled myself. 'There's nothing to worry about now. You haven't met Stephen properly, have you? Mrs Bosemann . . . Stephen Maitland. Stephen . . . Mrs Bosemann.'

She pumped his hand up and down vigorously. 'Honey, I sure am glad to see *you*. Now, perhaps someone would tell me what all the excitement's been about!'

We sat at one of the tables beneath the cool shade of the beech trees and as briefly as possible Stephen told our story, and how much we owed her.

'If you hadn't gone back to check that Susan's message had been delivered, and then, when you found it hadn't and that I wasn't even at the hotel, hadn't persisted in finding me, Susan wouldn't be here now. Nor would I.'

For once Mrs Bosemann was speechless. Her jaw had dropped lower and lower and her eyes had grown rounder and rounder as Stephen had been talking, and now all she could say was: 'Well, I never. Who on earth would have thought . . . well, I never.'

'At any rate,' said Mr Bosemann, leaning back in his chair and puffing contentedly at a large cigar, 'at any rate it was nothing serious. Now, if you two people had *really* quarrelled that *would* have been something to get upset about!'

I kicked off my sandals and sat down on the grassy hillside. It was two days later and all the official statements had been taken. Stephen and I were free to leave Oberammergau whenever we liked. The hotel had given us a packed lunch and two bottles of the local wine and we had spent the morning driving leisurely past Lake Constance towards the French border. Just beyond Villingen we had pulled off the road and climbed up through thick, pine trees warm and spicy in the sun, to the grassy uplands where we sat eating our picnic and enjoying the view.

Far below us a river meandered gracefully between the gently sloping hills and the only sound was that of the birds singing and the occasional hum of a bee. We sat in companionable silence while we ate, and then Stephen said quietly, 'That's the Neckar.'

I sat up. 'Honestly? I'd no idea it flowed so far west.'

'Goose,' he said, ruffling my hair. 'This is where it starts. It springs up somewhere between here and Freudenstat.'

'And flows through Niedernhall . . . ' I stared down at its sunlit surface. 'This is how it all started. Sitting in the sunshine, eating a picnic, watching the river flowing far below.'

'But then,' said Stephen, 'you were by yourself. Now you have me to take care of you. And, oh, my darling, I promise you I shall take the greatest possible care of you.'

I knew he meant it.